MY
BROTHER'S
WAR

David Hill is an award-winning writer who lives in New
Plymouth in New Zealand. His many novels, stories and
plays for young adults have been translated into several
languages and published internationally.

David's acclaimed novel for teens *Coming Back* is also
available from Aurora Metro Books.

www.aurorametro.com

For all my uncles – D.H.

MY BROTHER'S WAR

DAVID HILL

AURORA METRO BOOKS

Published in the UK by Aurora Metro Books in 2015.
67 Grove Avenue, Twickenham TW1 4HX
www.aurorametro.com   info@aurorametro.com
My Brother's War by David Hill © copyright David Hill 2012.
First Published by the Penguin Group (NZ).
On page 79 Archie quotes the first line of an 1807 poem
by William Wordsworth, 'I Wandered Lonely as a Cloud'.
Map by Outline Draughting and Graphics Ltd

Aurora Metro Books would like to thank Neil Gregory, Richard Turk, Suzanne Mooney, Emma Lee Fitzgerald, Hinesh Pravin, Chantelle Jagannath and Russell Manning.

Printed in the UK by podww.com
ISBN 978-1-906582-63-0

The author acknowledges the help of
Archibald Baxter's superb memoir,
We Will Not Cease.

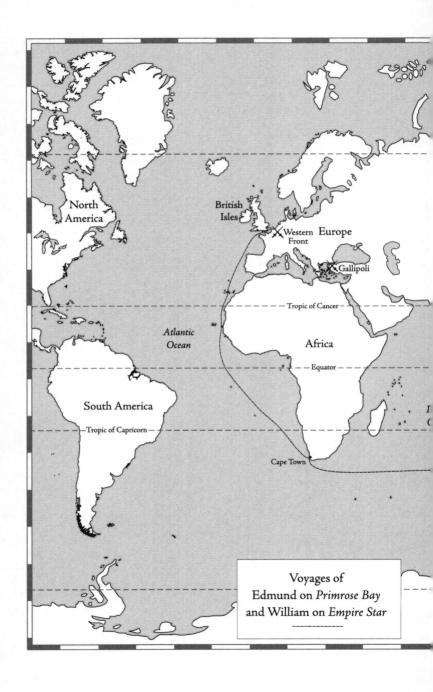

North America

British Isles

Western Front

Europe

Gallipoli

Tropic of Cancer

Atlantic Ocean

Africa

Equator

South America

Tropic of Capricorn

Cape Town

Voyages of
Edmund on *Primrose Bay*
and William on *Empire Star*

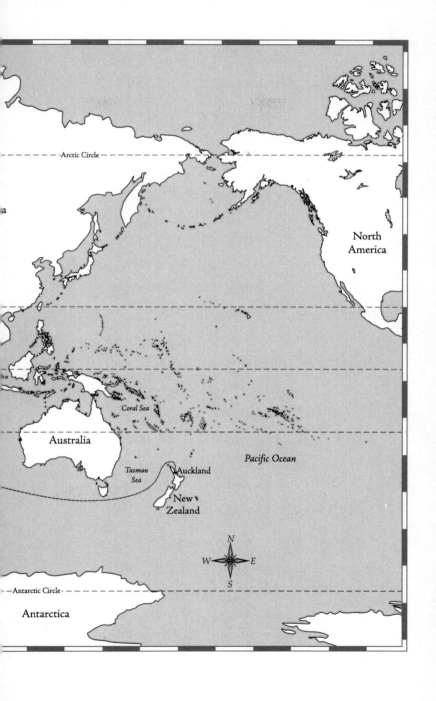

Glossary

CO	conscientious objector
CSM	Company Sergeant Major; an NCO in charge of a company of soldiers, especially in charge of ammunition in combat
dixie	a large iron cooking pot
duckboards	wooden slats joined together to form a path over muddy ground
howitzer	an artillery gun that fired shells in a high arc to destroy enemy defences
mess tin	a rectangular metal tin that was part of a soldier's mess kit (utensils for cooking and eating)
NCO	non-commissioned officer, an enlisted soldier who has authority over other soldiers
Lewis Gun	a light machine-gun
Mills Bomb	a type of hand grenade
pillbox	a small concrete fort, partly underground, used as an outpost
Zeppelin	a large German airship

PART I
AT FIRST

My Dear Mother,

Well, I've gone and done it. I've joined the Army!

Don't be angry at me, Mother dear. I know you were glad when I wasn't chosen in the ballot. But some of my friends were, and since they will be fighting for King and Country I want to do the same. I believe New Zealand must do her bit to support Britain against the Huns. I wanted to join up after our Kiwi soldiers had such a terrible time fighting against the Turks at Gallipoli, and now I've enlisted.

It wasn't just me. A lot of us at the factory have been feeling the same way. When Mr Parkinson heard us talking, he said, 'You go ahead, boys. The British Empire needs you. Go down to the Drill Hall and give your names to the Recruiting Officer, then take the rest of the day off. If I was thirty years younger, I'd be with you.' So we gave him three cheers, and five of us went.

It was all a bit of a lark. At the Drill Hall, a sergeant took our names. Then he marched us down the road to where Mr Darney the lawyer has his office. It was like Military Training at school – except I think we marched better then!

Mr Darney was a witness while we all swore loyalty to King George V and the British Empire. Then the sergeant marched us back to the Drill Hall. Some girls came out of shops as we passed and called out 'Good on you, boys!', which made us all grin and stick our chests out.

But I'm not doing this just so girls can cheer me. I know Father would have wanted me to enlist. You've read in the newspapers about German soldiers burning Belgian people alive inside their houses after somebody shot at German troops. You've heard about Huns killing Belgian babies. We have to stop a country which behaves like that.

The sergeant said we will get our orders to report to training camp soon. I'll come home and spend time with you and Jessie before then. You can tell Edmund what I've done. I don't want to speak to him any more. He and I can't talk about the war without losing our tempers and shouting at each other. You already know that.

Yes, he's my brother, but his refusing to enlist, and his talk about all war being evil and wrong is just stupid. You've probably heard that some people are calling him a coward. Perhaps he is.

Anyway, I'm proud to think that I'll soon be doing my bit against the Hun. It will be a great adventure. I'll see the world. My love to you and Jessie. Tell her she doesn't have to salute her big brother when she sees him in uniform! My dear Mother, I feel so good now that I've finally signed up.

Your Loving Son,

William

Dearest Ma,

This letter is to tell you that four days ago I received a letter from the local Army Recruiting Officer. No, it didn't wish me a Happy Eighteenth Birthday! It ordered me to report for military training next week.

What did I write back? The same as I wrote to the Conscription Board when my name was chosen in the ballot. I said I won't be part of any military system, and I don't believe we should kill people just because our government tells us to. I said that I don't belong to a church, but I agree with the Bible: 'Thou shalt not kill' and 'Thou shalt love thy neighbour as thyself'.

Goodness me, I do sound serious, don't I? You'll be wondering, Is this really my younger son? The one who used to chase Jessie with a dead mouse, just to make his little sister scream?

Well, dear Ma, I'm VERY serious. I'm officially a CO now – a Conscientious Objector. 'Conchies', people call us. And worse names, but I won't make your ears burn with them!

Seriously, Ma, I hope I can be brave in the days ahead. I know there are others who feel the same as me, but I have no idea how many, as the newspapers won't print our letters or report our meetings.

I know I'll lose friends. Yesterday at the butcher's shop, Mr Hansen refused to serve me. He said he wasn't having anything to do with a coward. But then Mrs Hansen told him not to be silly, and sold me the meat I wanted. In fact, she gave me twice as much! You should have seen Mr Hansen's face. I nearly burst out laughing.

Mr Yee is very good to me as well; he says he'll always keep a job for me in his market garden.

Ma, I know William is angry with me. He's my older brother: I respect him and love him. I'm sorry the arguments he and I had about the war were so ugly. But I'll never agree with him that duty to King and Country must come first. I believe our duty to other human beings is more important. We mustn't make war on them.

You can already see how this war is twisting people's minds. A friend told me how one British newspaper reporter in Belgium found that the stories of German soldiers killing babies were all made up – there was no truth in them. And what happened? The newspaper wouldn't print his article; he lost his job; his fiancée broke off their engagement.

I am sorry Father is no longer there to support you, dear Ma. I think he'd have understood both me and William. I've been told by other men who have refused military service that the police will probably arrest me in a week or so. I'll send you a photograph of my cell!

Dearest Ma, my love to you and Jessie. Don't worry: I have no regrets over what I have chosen. I am doing what my heart tells me I must do.

Your Loving Son

Edmund

Edmund

On Monday morning, five days after he wrote to his mother, Edmund was hoeing lettuces in the market garden. He'd decided to work every hour Mr Yee offered him, so he could send some money to his mother and sister.

His mother earned a little by doing washing for some of the wealthy families nearby ('You mean rich people get their clothes dirty?' Edmund had joked to her), and Jessie had just been taken on full time at the hat shop. They would also receive a small payment from the government, because William had joined the Army and there was no man left at home to support them.

Edmund hoped the government payment wouldn't be stopped when he was arrested. He hoped his mother and sister wouldn't lose their jobs when people learned he was a conscientious objector. He'd heard of such things happening.

He was half way down the last row when Mr Yee called to him. 'Ed-mon!' When Edmund looked up, his boss was in the doorway of the big wooden shed. He beckoned to Edmund, then turned and went inside.

I suppose he wants a hand to get more boxes ready, Edmund decided. Monday was always busy in the market garden. Mr Yee had set out at 6 a.m. with his horse and cart to take the week's first vegetables to the greengrocer's. No shops were open on Sunday, of course. Edmund laid down his hoe and headed for the shed.

'Hello, boss,' he said as he came in. 'Here's your best worker. Your *only* worker.' His eyes were still dazzled from the sunlight outside, but he could see Mr Yee standing in the middle of the floor, facing him. No, it wasn't: the Chinaman was over by the far wall, looking frightened and suddenly old. The man facing Edmund was young, tall and broad-shouldered, wearing a dark-blue uniform and a dark-blue helmet. Edmund felt his stomach go heavy as he understood what was happening.

Another half-second, and he recognised the uniformed figure. 'Hello, Tim,' he greeted the constable. 'Never thought I'd be arrested by someone from my cricket team.'

The young policeman looked embarrassed. 'Are you Edmund Frederick Hayes?'

Edmund couldn't help grinning. 'Well, I was when I woke up this morning. Come on, Tim!'

A hand shoved him hard from behind. He staggered across the floor and almost collided with the constable. 'None of your conchie cheek here!' a voice grunted.

15

Edmund swung around. Another policeman stood there, a man he'd never seen before, older and heavier than Tim, neck swelling above his high uniform collar. His fists were half-clenched, and Edmund knew suddenly that this man would like to hit him. The stranger glared. 'Come on, then! Even you conchie cowards know your own names. Answer!'

The younger constable swallowed, then began again. 'Are you Edmund Freder—'

Edmund interrupted him. 'Yes. Yes, Tim, I am.'

'I – we have a warrant for your arrest, as a result of your refusal to obey a lawful written order under the Military Service Act of 1916.' Edmund's team-mate looked as if he'd sooner be facing the world's fastest bowler than having to do this.

'Hold your hands out!' As Edmund stood uncertainly, the older policeman grabbed his arms and pulled them straight out in front. Next minute, cold hard metal was around his wrists, squeezing them painfully. There was a *clack*, and he stared down at a pair of handcuffs, the steel pinching his flesh. Over by the wall, Mr Yee gasped, then stood still.

Edmund's heart was thudding. He made himself breathe deeply. 'You don't need those. I'm not going to run away.'

'Quiet!' The unknown constable thrust his face forward. 'That's all you conchies are good for – running away. Well, you won't be doing that for a while, you spineless coward. Now, move!'

A beefy hand grabbed Edmund's arm and hauled him towards the shed doorway. On a chair nearby, he saw the small suitcase he'd brought to work every day since he'd written his reply to the Conscription Board. In it were toothbrush, towel, spare clothes, books: ready for him to take when this happened. 'My case—' he said. 'Can I—'

'I said quiet!' The older policeman shoved him again. The younger one followed. As they came outside, into the bright blue morning where everything had changed, Edmund stopped and turned. He ignored the hand pushing at his chest, the angry face glaring at him. 'Mr Yee!' he called. 'My mother. She—'

'I go see her.' His boss looked small and scared, but he spoke firmly. 'I go now.' Then the burly constable spun Edmund around, clamped a hand on his shoulder and pushed him forward.

Thirty yards, and they reached the road. The grip on Edmund's shoulder tightened. 'I'm warning you,' the voice behind him went. 'Don't try any clever tricks. You won't be the first conchie who accidentally falls over and breaks his nose while resisting arrest.' He turned to the younger policeman. 'Where's the main road into town? We're going to take this yellow-belly where everyone can see him.'

But Edmund's team-mate shook his head. 'No. We'll go along the side roads. I believe him. He won't try to run away.'

The bigger man's face flushed red. 'You listen to me.

We'll—'

'No.' Tim's voice was quiet but determined. '*You* listen to *me*, or you find your own way into town. You don't know this place, so how's it going to look when you have to stop on every corner and tell people you're lost?'

Edmund's team-mate stood facing the other constable, jaw clenched. He looks just like when he bowls at cricket, Edmund thought. For a couple of seconds, he also thought he was going to see one policeman punch another. Then Mr Yee was there, holding Edmund's jacket and his suitcase from the chair. 'You take,' he said. 'You take. I tell mother.' He gazed at Edmund for a second, his dark eyes tired and sad. Then he turned away.

Tim took the suitcase. He draped the jacket over Edmund's wrists so it hid the handcuffs. The other policeman started to speak, but Tim pointed a finger at him. 'We do this the way I said, or you do it by yourself.' His companion glared, then gripped Edmund's arm and began striding forward.

They saw hardly anybody on the twenty-minute walk into town. Those they did meet looked puzzled, watched them pass, said nothing.

Edmund knew that Tim was leading them along the quietest, most deserted streets and paths he could find. The young constable walked beside him, saying little. As they approached the Drill Hall, he murmured to Edmund, 'I'll go and see your mother, too. Is there anyone else you want to tell?'

Edmund shook his head. He'd worked all this out in the weeks since he'd replied to the Conscription Board. 'No, thanks, Tim. I'm—'

The other policeman shouted, 'Prisoner will be silent!'

A woman beating rugs on her side fence stopped and stared.

Three soldiers with rifles and bayonets were waiting in the Drill Hall. Edmund recognised one of them: a friend of William's. The man kept his eyes on the floor.

One of the soldiers wore a corporal's stripes on his tunic. 'Are you Edmund Frank Hayes?'

Once again, Edmund couldn't hold back a half-smile. 'No. Sorry.'

The corporal looked startled.

'I'm Edmund *Frederick* Hayes,' Edmund told him. 'Edmund Frank was my grandfather. He died ten years ago; I don't think he'd be much use to you.'

One soldier started to grin, then quickly stopped. The corporal stared at the sheet of paper he held. 'Edmund Fr— Edmund Hayes, you are charged with failing to obey a lawful written order under the Military Service Act of 1916. We are here to take you into military custody.' He turned to the two police officers. 'We'll look after him now.'

'You're welcome to him,' the older constable grunted. He threw Edmund's jacket on the floor, seized his wrists and unlocked the handcuffs. Red welts stood out on the skin where the metal had dug in.

Tim bent, picked up the jacket and handed it and the small suitcase to Edmund. 'Good luck,' he said quietly. 'I'm sorry.' The two young men looked at each other; Tim nodded and left.

'Escort, form up!' At the corporal's order, the other two soldiers stepped forward, rifles and bayonets over their shoulders, and stood on either side of Edmund. The NCO moved across and opened the Drill Hall door. 'Escort and prisoner, quick march!' Next minute, they were out in the street, heading for the centre of town.

For the first few yards, it was almost like being back in school's Military Training. Edmund had always enjoyed marching with the brass band in those days, and he found his arms swinging and his steps matching the tramp of boots on either side of him, just as they had in his schooldays.

Then he realised what he was doing. He let his arms hang naturally and walked at a normal pace. But he kept his head up and he looked straight into the faces of everyone they passed.

There were many more people here, in the main shopping street. As he and the escort marched past the draper's, Edmund saw a group of well-dressed women staring at him. One was Mrs Twigg, the doctor's wife for whom his mother did washing. As soon as she met Edmund's eyes, she turned her back.

By the hotel, some young men began yelling 'Conchie! Conchie coward!' Edmund's fists clenched, but he kept his face still and gazed at them also. Then his breath caught: two of them were William's workmates from the factory; he'd met them at rugby a couple of times. They recognised him, too, and went silent.

There were jeers and boos from other people as well. An apple landed on the road, obviously aimed at Edmund, but nearly hitting one of the soldiers instead. The man jerked, clutched harder his rifle with its glittering bayonet. 'Steady!' the corporal barked, and they trod on.

Past the butcher's they went. Mr Hansen burst out of the door, began to yell something at Edmund. Mrs Hansen appeared, held onto his arm and spoke fiercely to him. The butcher stood scowling as they passed.

Then another man's voice called out, so loud that the soldiers jerked again. 'Well done, lad! Somewhere there's a mother glad that you won't be killing her boy!' Edmund stared into the bright morning sun, trying to see who had shouted. He couldn't make out anybody, but his head came up again, and his heart felt lighter.

They stopped outside an office building. 'Escort, order arms!' The two other soldiers brought their rifles down to their sides. 'All right, chum.' The NCO's voice was friendly enough. 'We're going in here. Be sensible about it.'

Two men sat at a table, in a front room full of dark books. One was in army uniform, the other wore a suit; Edmund had seen him around town. The three soldiers snapped to attention, and the corporal saluted. 'Prisoner under escort as instructed, sir!'

The man in uniform – an officer, Edmund realised – nodded. 'Stand easy, men.' The soldiers relaxed slightly, and the officer looked at Edmund. 'I'm sorry you had to be marched through the streets like that, Mr Hayes, but orders are orders. I'm Captain McGregor. This,' he nodded to the man in the suit, 'is Mr Darney. Mr Darney's a solicitor and he's here to make sure everything is done properly. Actually, I believe you had the pleasure of meeting Mr Hayes's elder bother just the other day, didn't you, Mr Darney?'

Edmund's stomach jumped. William? What was—? The solicitor nodded. 'He and some friends came in to take the Oath of Loyalty after they'd enlisted. A fine young man. Your family must be very proud of him, Mr Hayes.'

The two of them watched Edmund. He spoke and was glad to hear his words come clearly. 'Thank you. He *is* a fine young man, and we have always been proud of him.'

The officer nodded. 'Well, I'm sure your family want to be proud of you, too, Mr Hayes. After all, you've made your stand, and I don't doubt you believe in what you've been saying. Now, you can save yourself and your brother and mother a great deal of trouble. There's a uniform over there.' He nodded at a small table. 'Just say you'll wear it, and we can put all this unfortunate business behind us.'

Silence in the room. Edmund realised he was gazing at the neatly folded pile of khaki on the side table. His mind was spinning. Captain McGregor was right. He could save his family so much pain and worry. He could make his brother proud of him. He could do what so many other conscientious objectors had done: join the Army, but serve only as a stretcher-bearer, someone who didn't ever carry a gun. It would be perfectly sensible; nobody would ever blame him.

Nobody but himself. A glow, a firmness seemed to flood his whole body. He gazed steadily at the officer. 'No. Thank you, but I'll never serve in an organisation which aims to kill my fellow men.' He felt startled at his own words. I sound just like one of the pamphlets I've read, he thought.

Captain McGregor sighed. 'Think carefully, Mr

Hayes. A very difficult time lies ahead if you hold to these beliefs. And what will you achieve? You won't stop the war. Nobody will take any notice of you.'

He waited. The room was still; Edmund could hear the escort breathing. He said nothing, but he looked at the officer and the solicitor, and he shook his head.

A shrug from the officer. His voice sounded hard suddenly. 'As you wish. You have only yourself to blame for what follows.'

William

In the first days after William enlisted, people kept coming up to him in the street to shake his hand. The whole town seemed to know about it. Women smiled at him. Two pretty girls in big flowered hats whispered to each other, rushed up and kissed him on the cheek, then hurried away giggling. William didn't mind that at all.

Men invited him into the hotel for drinks, and he had to find ways of refusing. 'Sorry, but I have to be at work,' he told them. 'The factory is short-handed because of all the blokes who've already joined the forces.'

It was true. He didn't know how Mr Parkinson would manage, now that another bunch of them had signed up. He'd heard people talking about women taking over jobs while the men were away. Women working in factories? It made William laugh just to think about it.

There were some things he didn't enjoy. 'You're heroes, blokes like you,' people told him. William shook his head. The New Zealanders who'd fought at Gallipoli, battling the Turks on bare, high ridges, going without food and water for days, surviving in trenches with their dead friends lying out in the open in front of them – they were the real heroes. Could he be like them when it came to battle? He didn't know.

Sometimes he lay awake at night, remembering stories he'd heard of strong men who threw themselves on the ground when the first shots cracked past, tried to dig themselves into the earth with their fingernails. Would he be one of them?

He didn't like the flags waving everywhere, either. Or the banners across streets and in house windows, reading:

THE ONLY GOOD GERMAN IS A DEAD
GERMAN ... SHOOT A HUN FOR ME, BOYS.

A woman's dress shop had a petticoat hanging outside its front door, and a sign:

MEN:
IF YOU DON'T SIGN UP TO FIGHT,
YOU SHOULD BE WEARING THIS!

A music teacher wrote to the paper saying she had ripped up all her music that was written by German composers. One of William's friends had heard of a man who had grabbed his neighbour's little dachshund, shouted that there was only one way to treat a dog with a Hun name, and threw it in the river.

Most of all, William didn't like thinking about Edmund. He knew his younger brother was opposed to the war and the Army. They'd argued about it for the last three years. 'You and your peculiar ideas!' William had

26

joked at first. 'You'll soon start thinking sensibly.'

Instead, the arguments grew fiercer and angrier, until their mother told them they weren't to talk about it at home. Now William didn't talk about anything to Edmund; he hadn't spoken to his younger brother for almost a year. I'm ashamed of him, he kept telling himself. Ashamed, yet unable to forget him.

The letter ordering William to report for military training came two weeks after he signed up. Before then, he had written two letters himself. One was to his mother and Jessie, with some money Mr Parkinson had given him. William hadn't wanted to take it: 'I've already cost you a lot by leaving the factory so suddenly.'

But the older man insisted. 'I'd go myself if I were thirty years younger,' he said again. 'This is the least I can do. And your womenfolk are going to need help without ... without a man to support them.' So he knows about Edmund, William realised.

27

The second letter was also for Jessie and his mother, but he left it with Mr Darney. 'I'll be proud to look after it,' the solicitor told William. It was a letter to be delivered to his sister and mother if he didn't come back alive from the war. It said how he loved them, how he didn't regret what he was doing, because everyone must do their bit against the evil Hun. He asked to be remembered to relatives and neighbours. He didn't mention Edmund.

Another person tried to give him money as well. When his landlady Mrs Purchas asked him to buy some meat at the butcher's, Mr Hansen wouldn't take the money, gave him twice as many chops as he'd asked for and tried to hand him some pound notes from the till as well. 'Good to see there's one son in your family who's not afraid to do his duty.'

William felt his face go hot. Edmund was wrong and foolish, and a shame to the three of them, but he was still his brother. He pushed the pound notes and his landlady's money back across the counter. 'No, thank you. Mrs Purchas wants to pay.'

It was the butcher's turn to go red. 'It's not for her – it's for you! We're proud of you!' He tried again to thrust the money into William's hand, but William shook his head, and said 'No, thank you' once more.

Mrs Hansen, who'd been watching silently, stepped forward. 'William is right. But take the extra chops, my boy. You young fellows have keen appetites. And give our good wishes to your family. *All* your family.'

As William left the shop, he saw husband and wife behind the counter. One waving his arms and shouting; the other staring silently into space.

Two of the other men from the factory, Herbert Blunden and Jack Kahui, had to report to the Drill Hall at the same time as William. A corporal greeted them and checked their names. 'Hayes?' he went to William. 'We had a bloke through here last week with that name. Relation of yours?' Then he seemed to remember something. He glanced at William's stony face and bent over the form he was filling in. Jack and Herbert gazed at the scuffed floorboards and said nothing.

A train took them to camp, picking up young men from stations all along the line as it steamed through the countryside. They still all wore their civilian clothes, and some of them grumbled about this. 'The girls love a uniform,' one red-headed bloke went.

'So why didn't you join a pipe band instead?' asked someone, and there was laughter through the carriage.

Their uniforms were waiting for them at camp: scratchy khaki trousers and tunics, khaki shirts, leather belts and straps with pouches hanging everywhere. 'These boots feel like they're made of lead!' the red-haired soldier grumbled.

'They are!' Jack Kahui grinned. 'If you run out of bullets, you fire your army boots at the enemy.'

They had to polish the heavy footwear every evening,

until they could see their faces reflected in the black leather. 'Though Heaven knows why you horrible little men want to see such an ugly sight!' roared Sergeant Molloy, the NCO in charge of William's platoon. They were issued with their lemon-squeezer hats: the stiff cloth ones that rose to a point in the middle with dents on either side, but they were allowed to wear those only on leave or on formal parades. The red-headed bloke, whose name was Jerry O'Brien, grumbled about that, too.

They marched every day. There was drill on the parade ground. Sergeant Molloy's voice started as a shout and rose to a bellow. 'Step off with the left foot! The *left!* Don't you horrible little men know your left from your right?'

They learned how to turn and about-turn, how to come to attention so exactly that thirty pairs of boots all crashed down on the ground at the same moment. It was boring and their feet ached, and it seemed nothing to do with stopping the Germans.

'Are we going to beat the Huns by marching over the top of them?' Jerry demanded.

'You can just *boot* them out of their trenches,' Jack told him. 'Or go "*Shoe*, you nasty Germans! *Shoe!*"'

There was marching on the roads, too. Marching that took them for miles, away from the straight lines of round canvas tents and square wooden buildings that were the training camp. They trudged along, packs on backs, rifles on shoulders, boots thudding through the dust. Sweat poured down their faces. Blisters swelled on their feet. They grumbled under their breath until, as they finally slogged back into camp, a brass band formed up ahead of them and marching music filled the air. Then William felt his head come up, his arms swing higher, and knew that every soldier around him was doing the same. After three weeks, he was fitter than he'd ever been in his life.

On one march, they passed a troop of cavalry, sitting high on their gleaming horses, rifles in long sheaths by their sides. There were calls and jokes from both sides. 'What's the weather like down there on the ground, lads?' 'Was that the horse talking, or the bloke on it? The horse looks more intelligent.' William had read in the papers how cavalry were little use in this war; how, in 1914, lines of them had charged the enemy, only to be shot down in hundreds by machine guns. Now they were kept mainly for reconnaissance.

By the end of the first month's training, they'd also started learning how to kill.

With their .303 rifles, they lay or knelt or stood at the butts, aiming, firing, pulling the bolt back to expel the used cartridge, ramming the bolt forward to insert the next round, aiming and firing again. They shot until their rifle barrels were too hot to touch, until their nostrils were full of the bitter smell of gunpowder, until they were so deaf that Sergeant Molloy had to shout into their faces before they could hear him.

They threw Mills Bombs, standing in waist-deep trenches dug into bare ground a mile from camp. With sweating hands, they slid the detonator into position beside the explosive-packed metal head. Then they gripped the wooden handle, stretched their arm back and swung it forward like a bowler in a cricket match, sending the bomb curving through the air to land as close as possible to a group of man-shaped wooden cut-outs stuck in the ground twenty yards away.

'Aim! Throw! Down!' the Training NCOs yelled. 'Aim! Throw! Down!' Three of them threw at a time, then crouched in the trenches as the bombs burst with an evil *CRACK!* Iron splinters flashed overhead and black smoke blew past. By the time the platoon of thirty men had all thrown, the wooden cut-outs were just fragments of shredded wood, scattered across the ground.

William couldn't throw a Mills Bomb without thinking of Edmund. His younger brother had been the cricketer of the family, the one who was good at all sorts of games and adventures, running faster and throwing further than William ever could. So why had he turned his back on this greatest adventure of all?

Mostly, though, William tried to keep Edmund out of his mind. He didn't know what was happening to his brother. 'I don't *want* to know,' he'd told his mother.

'If Edmund is in trouble because of his foolish conscientious objector views, then that's his problem. If everyone was like him, there would be no armies at all!' The last words echoed eerily in William's mind.

Bayonet practice gave him other things to think about. They stripped to the waist, fixed the slim, eighteen-inch-long steel blades to their rifles, and charged at sawdust-filled sacks hanging from posts or lying on the ground. They plunged their bayonets into the sacks, tore them out, plunged them in again. They screamed and yelled as the NCO in charge told them to. 'Louder! It's not a sack! It's a Hun! A filthy German. Kill him! Kill him!'

After half an hour, they were all panting, hearts pounding. Jack patted Jerry on the shoulder. 'Easy, chum. Calm down now.' William saw that the red-headed soldier's eyes were wild and staring. Here was one thing he never would – never could – describe to his mother and sister.

Rumours kept running through the camp. 'There's going to be a big attack in France,' one voice said. 'We'll all be shipped over to take part.'

'No,' said a second voice. 'We're going to the Eastern Front – to save the Russian armies from the Germans and the Austro-Hungarians.'

'No,' came a third voice. 'We're going to make another attack on Turkey – same place as the 1915 Gallipoli campaign.'

The corporal in the Uniform Store had fought at Gallipoli. He had only two fingers left on his right hand where a shell fragment had hit him. When he heard the last rumour, he shook his head. 'They won't go back there. That was a slaughter-house.' William listened and wondered again how he would handle battle when he faced it for the first time.

Other rumours talked of new weapons that would win the war before William and the others even finished their training. Enormous armoured machines called tanks, rolling forward on caterpillar treads, had crushed the enemy barbed wire, smashed concrete pillboxes, sent the Germans fleeing in terror. The Huns in their turn were using poisonous gas, firing shells full of it that turned men's skin yellow and rotted their lungs, so they died choking on their own blood.

Most incredible of all, aeroplanes from both sides were now fighting in the skies above France, shooting at one another with rifles and Lewis Guns, while the infantry stared up from their trenches below.

William didn't know what to believe. 'Just let me knock off a few Huns with my rifle and bayonet, and I'll be happy,' said red-haired Jerry. Some of the others murmured agreement. Some were silent.

At the end of their first month's training, they were given five days' leave. They put on their lemon-squeezer hats and marched to the railway station with the band playing, while the children of NCOs living in camp marched along beside them.

For the first two days at home, William felt strange and unsettled. His civilian clothes felt so light after his uniform and boots. He kept waiting for a bugle call to tell him when it was time to do things. He even found himself almost standing at attention while he talked to Jessie and his mother, until his sister burst out laughing and threw her arms around him.

'Oh, William, William! You really are a soldier now! I'll invite Violet and the other girls over so they can fall in love with you!' William pictured Jessie's chattering, bright-faced friends from the tennis club and realised he was blushing.

He felt strange also because of the things he couldn't talk about – not to his friends or those of Jessie's who did come over, even though dark-haired Violet Casey was quiet and sensible; not to the neighbours and relatives who came to congratulate him and wish him well.

The bayonet training was one of those things.

And the stories of poisonous gas, and men crushed to death by tanks or burned by terrible-sounding weapons called flame-throwers.

'It must be hard for you,' said Violet, as she handed him a cup of tea. 'You'll be thinking of what lies ahead.'

William nodded. 'I almost wish I were already in Europe.' Violet said nothing. William glanced at her dark eyes and hair. Suddenly he wasn't sure he wanted to be in Europe after all.

Most of all, William couldn't talk about Edmund. Nobody mentioned him, until lunch on his last day, when he and his mother and sister sat around the kitchen table, drinking tea, eating cold mutton and potatoes. William glanced at his watch, half-wishing he didn't have to go, half-longing to be gone, remembering what he'd said to Violet.

Finally, he spoke the words he hadn't thought he could. 'Have you heard anything of Edmund?'

His mother stood without a word and left the room. Jessie watched her go, then turned back to her brother. 'Yes. Yes, we've had a letter.'

PART 2

BEFORE SAILING

Dearest Ma,

Now don't be upset, Ma, but I'm in prison!

You never thought your younger son would say that, did you? No, it's not one of my jokes. I'm in Mt Eden Prison in Auckland.

The police arrested me at Mr Yee's and handed me over to the Army. I told the officer I wouldn't put on a uniform, so they gave me three days in the Drill Hall cells. When I still wouldn't accept military orders, I was returned to the police and sentenced to twelve weeks' hard labour for 'disobeying a lawful military command'. The Army and the police like me so much that they've both invited me to stay in their prisons.

Don't be downhearted, Ma. I'm not. I had an interesting free trip to Auckland in the train! I saw some scenery I'd never seen before. I'm working in the prison quarry, helping break stones to make new roads. Hard labour? It's labour, but it's not too hard. It's good to work in the fresh air, almost like being in the market garden in some ways.

I've met so many other chaps who feel the way I do about war. A lot of COs have been sent here. I think the Army and the government don't know what to do with us!

Some of the fellows are objectors on religious grounds. Others are like me, and believe nobody has the right to order us to kill others.

There's an excellent bloke called Archie, quite a lot older than me. He was a keen member of his church, 'til he ran into trouble. What did he do? The minister was sick one day, and so Archie preached the sermon. He talked about a mother whose son was killed in battle while he tried to save another soldier. She kept his room at home exactly as it was and hoped he would somehow return to her. Then at the end of the sermon, Archie said it was a German mother and her son he was talking about. Isn't that amazing?

But people in the church complained, and he was asked to leave. The funny thing is, I'd already met him earlier.

I'll tell you how it happened, sometime.

The food here isn't as good as your cooking, dear Ma. The clothes are a bit strange, too – I wear a suit all the time! It's nothing like the suits that men in town wear. It's too big for me, and it's brown, with black arrows painted all over it. I almost burst out laughing when I saw other chaps wearing them. They looked as if they were going to some strange fancy-dress party.

The other prisoners include all sorts of blokes. I've made friends with a thief and had a few laughs with a drunk! No, Ma, I'm not getting into bad habits. Not any new bad habits, anyway. Seriously, though, there are some fine chaps here, although life has treated them badly.

Dearest Ma, I don't know what the future holds for me. I don't know how often I'll be able to write to you. If any parts of this letter have been blacked out, it's because the prison censors feel some details should be kept secret. (Serve me right if this paragraph gets blacked out.)

It was wonderful to receive your letter. I read it every night before they turn our lights out – at 8.00 p.m.; I live very healthy hours here! I'm so pleased Jessie is enjoying the hat shop. And congratulations to her on almost winning the tennis club singles.

I'm so pleased to hear that Mr Yee is bringing you vegetables. He is a good, kind man. I believe most people are kind, if you treat them the right way. I feel more and more that I have made the right decision about not fighting.

Do tell me any news of William. We've made very different choices, but it saddens me that there has been bad feeling between us. If he ever asks about me, please tell him that.

All my love to you and my little (but not for much longer, it sounds) sister.

Your Loving Son

Edmund

Edmund

In Mr Darney's office, Captain McGregor spoke again. 'I'll ask you one more time, Hayes.' (The 'Mr' had vanished.) 'Will you put on that uniform?'

Once more, Edmund shook his head. 'No.'

The officer turned to Mr Darney. 'The prisoner has refused a lawful order. Under the authority vested in me by the Military Service Act, he is sentenced to three days' solitary confinement, with bread and water.'

The solicitor nodded. 'Take him away!' snapped Captain McGregor. The corporal saluted, shouted 'Escort, form up!', and the other two soldiers, still with rifles and bayonets, stamped into position on either side of Edmund. 'Quick march!' the NCO ordered.

The moment they were out in the street, a voice began screaming at Edmund. A woman, thin and haggard, in a long black dress. 'Coward! Conchie coward! My son was killed, while you sneak around at home, you filthy little coward!'

She began rushing towards Edmund, hands lifted as though she was going to tear his face, but the corporal seized her. 'Come on, Mrs Fitzgerald. You know you can't behave like this. People are starting to complain. Calm down.'

Two other women came hurrying up. They put their

arms around the figure in black, who dropped her hands and began to wail. 'Come along, Rose,' one of them murmured. 'Come along with us, love.'

The escort and Edmund watched as the woman was led away, still weeping and moaning. Other people had come into the street to see what was happening. Some glared at Edmund. Some shook their heads. He realised his back was prickling and his heart thumping.

'Son shot at Gallipoli,' the NCO said. He stared at Edmund for a second. 'You can't blame her for hating people like you, lad. Right – quick march!' They moved on, Edmund walking at his own pace, keeping his head up as he had done before, wondering what would happen to him.

Back at the Drill Hall, a different NCO waited, a sergeant with a droopy grey moustache. He scowled at Edmund. 'This the conchie?'

The corporal answered stiffly. 'The prisoner Hayes has been sentenced to three days' solitary confinement with bread and water. I'm delivering him into your custody.'

'What a pleasure,' sneered the sergeant. 'Bring him through.' He led them down a corridor to the end, where a steel door with a tiny barred grille faced them. 'Your hotel is ready, conchie,' he sneered again. 'In you go.' Edmund stepped inside. The door clashed shut behind him, a key turned, and he was alone in his cell.

A grey, square space, half the size of his boardinghouse bedroom. No bed. No chair or table. Nothing except the concrete floor and walls, an electric light bulb glowing feebly behind another grille in the ceiling, and a chipped metal bucket in one corner. Edmund moved forward to look into it, then stepped back, face twisted in disgust. Whoever had been there before him had used the bucket as a toilet, and it was still half-full.

He stood against the far wall, trying to breathe steadily. After a few minutes, he went to the door and yelled through the bars. 'Hey! Hey!'

It was nearly five minutes before the grey-moustached sergeant appeared, still scowling. 'Stop your noise!'

'The toilet bucket hasn't been emptied,' Edmund told him. 'It stinks.'

The sergeant sneered once more. 'Smells like a conchie smells. You can live with it.'

'Nobody should have to live like this!' Edmund felt surprise at his own anger. 'Take it away, please, or I'll tip it through the grille.'

'You'll do nothing of the kind!' the NCO's voice rose to a yell. 'You'll stay there and keep your mouth—'

'What's going on here?' Another voice spoke from along the corridor. 'Sergeant Greene?'

The sergeant snapped to attention. 'Prisoner refuses to obey an order, sir.'

'I haven't been given an order.' Edmund raised his voice. 'The toilet bucket in the cell hasn't been emptied.

It smells utterly foul.'

He couldn't see the officer – as he guessed it was – but the reply came quickly. 'That should have been done when the previous prisoner was released. See to it, please, Sergeant Greene.'

'Sir!' As the NCO turned away, his eyes met Edmund's through the grille. Edmund knew he'd made an enemy.

For the rest of the day, there was nothing to do but sit on the concrete floor, or pace up and down. Three steps across the cell; three steps back. Edmund thought of all that had happened since he had arrived at the market garden that morning. Only that morning? It felt as though days had passed. Mr Yee calling him to the shed. Tim and the other policeman. The handcuffs. The walk to the Drill Hall, and then the escort to where Mr Darney and Captain McGregor waited. The people jeering at him. The man who'd called out 'Well done, lad' – who was he? The march back to this cell, and poor grieving Mrs Fitzgerald.

Well, he reminded himself, now it's all begun. Now you'll see how brave you are . . . or aren't. Ma, Edmund thought suddenly. Has she heard what's happening? One son willing to fight and be killed; one son willing to go to prison. Big brother and I haven't made it easy for you.

At 6 p.m., he heard footsteps down the corridor. A voice shouted: 'Prisoner, stand against the wall!' The door opened. One soldier stood holding a battered tin tray, while a second pointed a rifle at Edmund. The tray was thrust into his hands, the door clanged shut, a key turned, and he was alone again.

Edmund gazed at the jug of water and four thick slices of bread. 'Oh, Ma,' he sighed. 'This doesn't look much like your home cooking.' He placed the tray on the ground, sat down on the chilly concrete and began to eat.

At 7 p.m., the two soldiers appeared again. The tray was taken away. A thin mattress and one grey blanket were tossed into the cell. Fifteen minutes later, the bulb in the ceiling went dark.

Edmund didn't sleep much. He was cold. He could feel the hard floor through the worn mattress. But mostly, his mind churned with more pictures from the day. The policeman's meaty hand on his shoulder; the tramp of boots and the glitter of bayonets beside him. When would he be free to walk where he wanted again?

Voices called and feet clomped in the corridor at 5.30 a.m. Two different soldiers ordered him to put his blanket, mattress and toilet bucket outside the door. One passed him another tray with bread and water, and said, 'There you are, chum. Two-course meal.'

'Of *course*,' Edmund managed to joke. The soldiers grinned, and Edmund felt better. He was going to meet friendly faces and unfriendly ones, he knew that now. 'Sorry for the trouble,' he added.

The soldier who had handed him the tray shrugged. 'No trouble, pal. As long as you behave yourself.'

The tray was taken away half an hour later. I must exercise, Edmund told himself. He began pacing across his cell again. Three steps – turn. Three steps – turn. He could hear voices from somewhere in the Drill Hall. Wouldn't it be strange if William were there? If his brother knew he was here in the cells, what would he do? Ignore me, Edmund supposed.

Boots marched down the corridor. A key screeched in the lock. 'Prisoner outside!' It was Sergeant Greene.

When Edmund stepped out of his cell, the sergeant pushed a bucket and stiff brush at him. 'Scrub the corridor floor!' An armed soldier stood nearby, looking uncomfortable.

Edmund gazed at the brush and bucket. 'Is this a military order?'

'Don't get smart with me, conchie!' The NCO's face went tight. 'Scrub the floor!'

Edmund shook his head. 'I won't obey any army

orders.'

The NCO stepped forward, lifted his fist. He glared into Edmund's face. Then – 'Into your cell!' he shouted.

The next two days were much the same. Bread and water, pacing the cell floor, the thin mattress and blanket brought at night-time, then taken away in the morning. The orders which he refused to obey. On the third morning, when Sergeant Greene appeared, Edmund said, 'I'd like to write to my mother.'

'Wait 'til they lead you out to face the firing squad,' Sergeant Greene grunted. 'Maybe they'll give you time to send a postcard then.'

Although he didn't believe the NCO, Edmund's back went cold. 'Will the Army pay for the stamp?' he made himself say. The sergeant glared and stomped away.

Later that day – Thursday – it was hard to keep track of the days with no calendar or newspaper – he was handed a sliver of yellow soap and a rough towel. 'Smarten yourself up. You're going before an officer.'

Captain McGregor again? No, the man seated at the table when two soldiers led Edmund into the room was not much older than himself and wore the two shoulder pips of a lieutenant. 'Prisoner Hayes, sir!' rapped the sergeant. The lieutenant nodded. 'At ease.' Edmund knew that voice; it had told the sergeant to empty the toilet bucket.

The two young men gazed at each other. 'Do you

have any complaints about your treatment in the cells, Hayes?' Edmund thought of the bread and water, and half-smiled. 'No.'

The officer seemed to read his mind. His own lips curved for a second. 'Are you now willing to obey military orders?'

This time, Edmund didn't even have to think. 'No.'

The young lieutenant didn't seem surprised. 'In that case, you will be handed over to the civil authorities. Their standard sentence for refusal to comply with the Military Service Act is twelve weeks' hard labour.' He paused, then spoke to Sergeant Greene. 'There is no need to take the prisoner away from here until it is dark. See that he is given proper food before then.' Another pause, then to Edmund: 'Good luck.'

An escort took Edmund to the Auckland train after his evening meal. The streets were almost empty, and Edmund felt grateful to the lieutenant. A middle-aged corporal and another soldier boarded the train with him. 'Now,' said the corporal. 'You promise us you'll be good, and we won't need any nonsense with handcuffs.'

Edmund remembered the steel rings biting into his wrists as they left Mr Yee's and nodded. 'I'll behave.'

They reached Auckland just after dawn. Another

escort was waiting on the platform and marched Edmund for half an hour past still-closed shops and businesses to Mt Eden Prison. A few people stopped to watch, but there were no jeers or yells.

Down a short street of houses, and the dark stone walls rose in front of them. Edmund had heard of the prison, even made jokes with friends about it. Now a small steel door set in a larger one opened, clanged behind him, and he was inside.

In a cold room with a long wooden table, he took off his clothes and was given a brown prison uniform two sizes too large, patterned with black arrows. Scratchy underwear and socks, a pair of badly fitting boots, and that was all. A guard led him along concrete-floored corridors and stopped in front of a door made from metal bars. 'Hooper?' he called. 'You've got company.'

A man rose from the bottom bunk as Edmund stepped in. He was in his forties, short and round, with hair starting to turn grey. He looked at Edmund, looked again and smiled. 'I know you.'

Edmund stared at him. He'd never seen the man before. But he'd heard him. He'd heard him call encouragement on Monday, as Edmund was marched through the streets of his town to the Drill Hall.

'Half of the people in the church I belonged to – once – they said I was right,' Archie Hooper explained later that day, when Edmund asked about his sermon. 'The second half wanted me thrown in jail, or hanged as a traitor. When I kept writing letters against the war to the newspaper, the second half got their wish. Well, not the hanging – so far.'

Edmund grinned. 'I haven't written any letters. I wouldn't know what to say. I just remember how when war was declared, my Ma said "Heaven help the young men – *all* the young men." And that made me decide I'm not going to hurt or kill someone just because our government says we have to.'

Archie put a hand on his cellmate's shoulder. 'None of my letters said it as well as that.'

On the first night, Archie showed Edmund how to lay out his blankets – two of them this time – to be most comfortable. 'Give them a good shake. They're always stiff; they bake them in big ovens to get rid of lice and suchlike beasties.' He told him about the other prisoners. 'Burglars, forgers, swindlers, horse-stealers. And there's half a dozen other COs here at least. You're among friends, young Edmund.'

'You mean the crooks or the COs?' Edmund asked.

As his twelve weeks began to pass, Edmund met the other prisoners and made friends with many. Jimmy the old alcoholic, who got drunk and stole a police horse, spent a month in prison promising he'd never touch the grog again, was released, got drunk again and stole the same police horse. Ned, who lit fires in rubbish tins because he liked watching things burn. Roland, who pretended to be a Russian prince and fooled people into giving him money.

He worked with them in the prison quarry, breaking up rocks with a sledgehammer until they were small enough to spread on new roads, then loading them onto big, horse-drawn carts. As he watched the horses plod patiently out through the prison gates, Edmund sometimes yearned to be back in the market garden, under the sky, away from cold stone walls.

He told Archie about his former job. 'A Chinaman?' Archie asked. 'How do people treat him?'

Edmund thought of the store owner who refused to buy Mr Yee's vegetables. 'No yellow man's stuff here!' The children who sometimes yelled 'Ching-Chong-Chinaman!' as they passed. 'Some are good. Some aren't,' he told Archie.

His new friend nodded. 'War isn't the only time people behave badly.'

More days passed. Edmund's hands blistered, then grew hard. His back ached, then grew strong. The prison food was boring and greasy and often lukewarm. The tea was weak, with watered-down milk. He ate and drank, and longed for his mother's meals.

There were other COs in the prison, as Archie had said. Three of them were from the same family and the same church, thin silent men who never smiled and who ignored Edmund when he spoke to them. 'Don't go thinking that all conchies are nice blokes,' Archie laughed, when he heard about it. 'Some of them agree with us about not fighting, but ones like that still think we're going to Hell.'

One CO was a blacksmith; one was a farmer; one was a steeplejack. 'A bloke told me I was a coward, so I invited him to climb a hundred-foot-high chimney with me,' Cedric the steeplejack grinned.

When they could, they talked together about their refusal to fight. Doug the farmer and Basil the blacksmith thought they might agree to serve as stretcher-bearers, but they were worried about obeying military orders.

Archie looked thoughtful. 'You do what you believe is right. That's why we're here. But be careful. The Army has clever ways of getting you on their side.'

Sometimes the prison wardens let them talk together. Sometimes they kept them apart. 'The government doesn't want us finding out how many others think like us,' Archie said. 'They're afraid it might be catching.' He was in the cell after dinner (pale stew, a hunk of stale bread, a mug of weak tea), lying on the bottom bunk and talking to Edmund, who was stretched out on the top one. 'Don't know why they've left us two together. Maybe they think I'm too old for anyone to listen to me – and you're too young.'

Edmund pretended to be indignant. 'Young? I'm eighteen, remember . . . just.'

Some prisoners wouldn't talk to Edmund or the other COs. When one heard why Archie was in prison, he spat in the older man's face. Archie wiped his cheek calmly. 'Would you like me better if I killed people?' he asked the prisoner.

Edmund didn't tell Archie about William. The anger between him and his brother was still too raw in his mind. But they talked about what might lie ahead. 'The Army haven't finished with us yet, lad. They've hardly started.' The older man gave Edmund arguments to use against people who believed in war, taught him to write letters in his head so he could still 'talk' to family and friends. Edmund was allowed to write and receive just one letter a month.

53

Life in prison was grey. Grey walls, grey rocks in the quarry, grey floors, grey stew, grey light in the corridors, grey feelings. 'Is my hair turning grey?' Edmund asked the others one day, and they looked surprised. But in spite of his jokes, he knew Archie was right. The Army – and the government – hadn't finished with him.

There were bad times ahead. Would he be able to face them?

Rumours and half-news filled the prison. Russia's armies had collapsed, and the country was torn by revolution. The Germans were going to invade England by submarines. New Zealand troops were taking part in a huge attack in France. Edmund wondered if William was there. His mother hadn't mentioned him in her letters.

Then they began to hear about being taken to Europe.

Dear Jessie,

I'm writing to you at the hat shop (you can tell the others there that it's a letter from a gentleman admirer if you like!), because I want to explain the things I said after you told me about Edmund's letter from prison. And because I don't want Mother to read this and be upset.

I don't believe I will ever agree with Edmund's views about war. If everyone acted like him, who would fight the Hun? How would we stop other countries from behaving like Germany – and Austro-Hungary and Turkey? Dear Sis, sometimes there are nations or people who do evil things, and the only way to stop them is to fight.

Edmund is not the only one who hates the idea of killing people. I hope I never have to do so. But I will if I have to, to protect our King and British Empire, our country, and you and Mother. Nearly all the chaps here feel the same way. They'd sooner be living their own lives, but they know they must do their duty.

I've heard of men who hate war just as much as Edmund, and who refuse weapons, the way he does. But they are willing to put on a uniform and act as a stretcher-bearer. Or else they work in the pioneer battalions, making roads and building bridges. Why won't Edmund do that? Because he won't fight, some other man has to go in his place and run the risk of being killed.

I don't believe he is a coward, but I believe he is foolish and wrong. Am I ashamed of him? Yes, I'm ashamed of the worry he has caused you and Mother. I'm ashamed of what he has done to the honour of our family.

I'm proud of you, Jessie. I know that Father would be proud of you if he were still alive. I wonder what he would have said about Edmund? I know that Mother wants us all to be at peace and forgive one another.

But if I hadn't signed up, I just wouldn't be able to look people in the eye. And there are so many great chaps here, Sis. I can't let them down. Look after Mother and yourself. I'll write again as soon as I can.

Your Loving Brother

William

William

William hadn't said anything untrue to Jessie. But he didn't tell her how a lot of the soldiers training with him had volunteered for the Army mainly because they hoped it would be an adventure. He remembered using the same words when he wrote to his mother and sister after enlisting.

'Joined up because I wanted to see the world,' one of 3 Platoon told him. Another laughed: 'I joined to get away from the wife.' A third grunted: 'The police arrested me for being drunk again. The magistrate told me I could enlist in the Army or go to jail.'

One night as he lay awake and other chaps snored around him, William found himself wondering if all armies were like that. Even the Germans. No. No, the Huns were evil. Otherwise what were he and his friends fighting for? He sighed. He wished his father were still here to give him advice. What *would* he have said about his younger son?

William had become friends with the red-headed Jerry. You couldn't see much of the red now, thanks to the stubbly haircuts they'd been given. 'You'll be glad of those haircuts in the trenches,' smirked the corporal who'd been at Gallipoli. 'Makes it easier to find the lice.'

Jerry had been a shearer before he enlisted and he'd

never been further than the nearest town. 'The blokes say we might get to London!' he exclaimed. 'I wonder if we'll see the King? Do you think he wears his crown at home? And I want to see the Tower of London. They should lock all the conchies up there 'til the war's over. Then they should have to lick the soldiers' boots 'til they're allowed out!'

'Calm down, young feller,' Jack chuckled. William said nothing. Jerry was a kind-hearted chap, under all his talk.

Their training went on. More rifle practice. More bayonet practice and Mills Bomb practice.

There was a scary moment when one of William's 3 Platoon let go of a bomb's wooden handle too soon, and it flew almost straight up in the air to land just in front of them. Everyone hurled themselves down in the dirt of the trench bottom, while the blast echoed overhead and slivers of metal whined past. Sergeant Molloy seized the thrower by his ear, pulled him up and growled, 'Next time, my lad, we'll tie you to the bomb and throw *both* of you at the enemy!'

William enjoyed the shooting, although after every practice his ears rang and his shoulder hurt from the slam of the rifle butt recoiling against it. He didn't enjoy learning to dig trenches, shovelling until there was a slit in the ground eight feet deep and five feet wide, with sandbags of dirt piled up in front for protection against enemy bullets.

'They say – that in France – there are trenches – a hundred miles long,' panted Herbert, as he and William and Jack dug and dug one day. Jerry, who was supposed to be looking through a periscope to make sure no enemy attack was coming, grinned down at them. 'You'll all be great gardeners when the war's over.'

Gardening made William think of Edmund. He said nothing, and dug harder.

They learned to string barbed wire on wooden stakes in front of their trenches. It was nothing like the barbed wire William had seen on farm fences. This had iron blades as big as a man's thumb.

One afternoon, they all lay on the ground while machine-guns and rifles fired just a few feet above their heads. It was meant to get them used to the whine and crack of bullets through the air. Jerry lay and whistled. The rest of them lay and listened.

Then they all jerked and stared as a man just along from Herbert, a tall, slim fellow who didn't talk much, began gasping and shouting 'No! No! Let me go!' He started struggling to his feet, still yelling, while the bullets sped overhead. Three men dragged him down. Sergeant Molloy blew a shrill blast on his whistle; the firing stopped, and the man was led away. Next morning, his gear and he were gone from the camp.

'Better off without cowards like that,' one man

muttered when they heard. But Herbert shook his head. 'None of us know how brave we'll be when the real thing comes.' Thank goodness, William thought. Someone else feels the same.

In the second month, they began practising attack skills. They swarmed up ladders out of their trenches when their platoon officer Mr Gowing blew a whistle, and rushed through clear lanes in their own barbed wire. They spread out into small groups, each man five yards from the next, so a shell would cause as few casualties as possible. Then they began advancing towards where the enemy would be.

'Keep apart!' NCOs yelled. 'Fast walk! Bayonets ready! Scan the ground!'

If it were a real battle, their artillery would be laying down a rolling barrage fifty yards in front of them, they were told – a wall of fire and flying steel, killing any enemy who tried to stand up in it, moving forward at the same speed as them.

But since this was a practice, there was no real artillery. ('Shells cost too much,' grunted Jack.) Instead, there were a few soldiers walking along, fifty yards in front, waving red flags and shouting 'Bang! Bang!' As they advanced, rifles and bayonets held diagonally across their bodies, William heard a snorting sound beside him. It was Jerry, trying not to laugh.

They did see and hear real artillery, though.

The morning after their attack practice, they marched for two hours to a valley where four big guns stood pointing across a barren area of sand and scrubby bushes.

For thirty minutes, they stood just behind the guns as they crashed and bellowed, lurching back on their huge wheels after each shot, while the gun-crews swarmed around them, heaving the next shell into the breech, clanging it shut, checking the range and firing again. A mile away down the valley, geysers of dirt and smoke burst into the air.

'These are just babies,' an NCO said. 'There are guns mounted on railway lines that can fire a shell thirty miles.'

As the days passed, they became browner and fitter and more eager to do their bit. Over in Europe, the third winter of the war was ending. The newspapers described how water in shell-holes turned to ice, and how men in the trenches stood up to their knees in snow or icy slush. 'It's the Army way of cooling down hot-headed blokes like you,' Jack told Jerry, who laughed.

Just before they went home for their next leave, they practised a night attack. Flares rose and burst in the black sky, throwing weird red or green light over the ground. Machine-guns fired in the air, to make everything as realistic as possible. Men lost their way in the dark, got caught in barbed wire, tripped and stumbled, attacked their own side by mistake.

'Surrender!' voices shouted. 'But I'm one of yours!' other voices shouted back. 'Hey, we're over here!' the enemy called.

'If I were the Germans, I'd be terrified by what happened tonight,' Sergeant Molloy snarled as they marched yawning back to camp at 2 a.m. 'Terrified you horrible little men might want to be on *my* side!'

The second leave was good. William worked in the garden, so there would be plenty of vegetables for his mother and Jessie after he was gone. 'The peas are good this year,' his sister said. 'And the potatoes,' went his mother. Neither of them spoke of the war.

Friends and relatives visited again, but they didn't fuss over him too much, and he was grateful for that. When one of Jessie's tennis friends began to weep at the thought of William being killed or wounded, quiet, dark-haired Violet took the girl outside. 'Thank you,' William told her later.

Violet looked at him and smiled. 'I shall miss you when you've gone,' she said. They were both silent for a minute. 'Jessie and your mother are being very brave,' the young woman went on. 'We all admire them. We admire *you* – and your brother.' William didn't know what to say.

His mother and sister had received a letter each

month from Edmund while he was in prison. 'He's fit and well,' Jessie said. 'His jail sentence is nearly finished but he doesn't know what will happen to him next. More time in prison, or in an army jail, he thinks. We couldn't read parts of his letter; the censors had blacked them out.'

William nodded. His foolish, foolish younger brother! Then he remembered Violet's last words and was silent.

Yes, it was good to be home, and he felt tears in his own eyes on the morning he left. His sister and mother were also trying hard not to cry. 'We'll be all right, my dear son,' his mother told him. 'Make sure that you are, too.' Jessie hugged him hard. 'Violet sends her best wishes,' she said, and gave him a secret smile. Once again, William didn't know what to say.

In some ways, he felt as he had after his other leave. He was pleased to be back in camp. They'd trained and trained, and now they wanted to show what they could do.

A major gave them a lecture on what New Zealand and Great Britain and their allies were fighting for. 'We didn't start this scrap,' he told the rows of seated men in their khaki uniforms. 'Britain came to the defence of gallant little Belgium when the Huns invaded there. Where Britain goes, the British Empire goes. New Zealand was the first country in the whole Empire to declare war on Germany. Doesn't that make you chaps feel proud?'

Actually, William felt embarrassed at the way the major went on. Beside him, Jerry and Herbert and Jack shifted on the hard wooden benches and stared at the floor.

But they joined in the three cheers for King George V that they were ordered to give at the end. 'Remember God is on our side!' were the major's final words. As they filed out, someone grunted, 'I bet some German officer's telling a bunch of Hun soldiers right now that God's on *their* side.'

Rumours and news kept flowing through the camp. 'The Germans are moving all their troops west now the Russians have surrendered,' went voice one. 'They're preparing to launch a huge attack.'

'No, the Russian armies haven't surrendered,' went voice two. 'They're being taken on hundreds of ships to Scotland, and marching all the way down through England, so they can sail across to France and help crush the Huns.'

'The United States are going to enter the war on Great Britain's side,' went voice three. 'No, the United States are going to stay neutral,' went voice four.

'There are huge new aeroplanes landing soldiers behind German lines, so the Huns can be attacked from both sides,' went voices five and six. William knew this last story must be false; aeroplanes would never be able to do that.

Then came something that started even more rumours flying. Every soldier in camp was asked if he could swim. This could mean only one thing, everyone agreed. Very soon, they were going to be on a ship. The time for training had finished. The time for real fighting was about to begin.

PART 3
ON SHIP

Dearest Ma,

I don't know if you will get this. I'm scribbling it in my cell, before I am shipped to Europe.

How do I know I'm going there? Another CO was marched down to the wharf yesterday. Then they found they were a day early, and so they had to bring him back again! He told the rest of us what's happening.

We'd already guessed, anyway. The religious objectors were moved from the prison last week. They're all going to work on a farm, somewhere in the South Island. Then, two days ago, Archie was taken away.

When I came back from the quarry, his blanket and washing gear were gone. Nobody knows where he is. I think the Army and government realise what a wonderful speaker and thinker he is, so they've moved him to some place where he can't make more people see the evils of war.

Dear Ma, I suppose they will take us to the battlefield and try to make us fight. Will I do so? Never. My mind is absolutely made up.

I'll try to hand this letter to someone who can send it to you. Bless you, dear Ma, and you, my little (ha-ha!) sister. Tell William that I think of him with much affection.

Your Loving Son

Edmund

Edmund

He wasn't taken straight to the ship. He was taken first to the same cold room with the long wooden table where he'd been given his prison uniform twelve weeks ago. His own clothes were handed back to him and he put them on. Then he was led to another room, where an escort of two armed soldiers and a corporal waited for him. Edmund hadn't seen any of them before.

A couple of prisoners shook his hand as he made his way back down the corridor. Jimmy, the old alcoholic, looked as though he was going to cry. 'Be careful, sonny,' he mumbled. 'Be careful.' None of the other COs were there; the prison was definitely keeping them apart.

Once more he was marched through the streets. The gloomy stone walls of Mt Eden Prison dwindled behind him. How bright everyone's clothes look, he thought. And mine feel so light! Even the men in their work clothes looked well-dressed after the prison uniform. His army escort seemed young: Edmund knew he'd grown stronger and taller while he was in prison.

A couple of voices yelled out as he and the escort passed. 'Conchie coward! Spineless traitor!' Edmund remembered Archie's reply to the prisoner who abused him: 'Would you like me more if I went out and killed someone?' He kept his mouth closed, but looked steadily back at everyone.

His stomach lurched suddenly, as he saw a weeping woman standing and watching them pass. Ma! No. No, it wasn't. How could it be? But just thinking of her and Jessie brought tears into his own eyes.

At an army office fifteen minutes' march away, an officer sat behind a table. Another major, a plump black-haired man about Archie's age, with a crown on each shoulder. I might not want anything to do with the Army, but I'm seeing plenty of it, Edmund decided. A folded uniform lay on the table, so he knew what was coming.

'Stand to attention for the officer!' barked the corporal. Edmund didn't. Instead, he nodded politely to the major. 'Good morning.'

The officer didn't return his greeting. Instead, he pointed to the uniform. 'I want you to put that on, Hayes.'

Edmund shook his head. 'I'm sorry. I will not.'

'Why?'

'I can't accept any organisation that orders men to kill other men.'

The major slammed his hand down on the table so hard that the escort all jumped. 'Have you no pride, Hayes? I have a son your age, and I'd sooner see him dead on the battlefield than have him shame his family like you!'

Edmund felt his face go hot. But he kept his voice as calm as he could. 'I *do* have pride – in the human race and in my conscience. I'm sorry *your* pride would let you kill your son in such a way.'

The major's face went dark with rage. 'I have no time to waste with cowards like you. Take him to the cells!'

It was another night of bread and water, a toilet bucket, a thin mattress and a single blanket. 'What will happen now?' he heard himself mutter out loud. Still aloud, he murmured, 'Be a man.' Yes, he thought. Be a very young, very frightened man.

The following morning, before it was properly light, he was marched to the ship.

Four soldiers escorted him this time, through still largely empty streets, past the clanging and hooting of the railway yards, down to the wharves. The man behind kept trying to trip him, so he would fall and look stupid. The first couple of times, Edmund thought it was accidental, then he heard a snigger.

He stopped, so suddenly that the soldiers beside him marched on for two steps before they realised, and the man behind thudded into him. 'Stop that, please,' Edmund said. 'I don't believe you were ordered to humiliate me.'

The man's face flushed and he began to mumble something. 'Don't be a fool, Walsh,' snapped the corporal. 'Just do your job.' They started off again, and Edmund could feel eyes drilling into his back.

The wharves were crowded with men, horses, railway engines. Two ships were moored at the wharf along which Edmund was marched, steel sides towering up until they blocked out the early morning sun. Troops were filing up the gangway of one, moving slowly under the weight of their gear. Edmund's escort led him in that direction. Maybe William is here, he thought. What if he sees me?

Primrose Bay read the name on the ship's stern. The corporal left Edmund and the other three soldiers, and strode up a gangway also. 'Now you'll see what real men do,' sneered the man who'd tried to trip him. 'Bet you're shivering in your boots, eh?'

Wharf workers passed by, carrying ropes or pushing trolleys. One of them, an older man, paused. 'Conscientious objector?' he asked quietly. Edmund nodded. 'Well done, son,' the wharf worker said. 'My own boy feels the same way. Stay strong.'

Edmund glanced sideways. His escort were leaning on their rifles, gazing up at the ship, talking and laughing. He pulled the letter he'd written out from his jacket. 'Can you post this?' he whispered. 'For my mother.

Her address is on it.'

The wharf worker slipped the paper into his shirt pocket. He nodded to Edmund and moved on.

The corporal returned with a bald-headed sergeant. 'All right, young Hayes. No funny business,' grunted the sergeant. 'Up here.' He pointed to the nearest gangway. Next minute, Edmund was climbing up it. He was no longer on New Zealand soil.

Soldiers crowding the decks watched as he was led to a flight of stairs. Down inside the ship Edmund and the sergeant went, then still further down, then along a narrow steel corridor smelling of warm oil, paint and sea-water.

They stopped outside a steel door with a grille across its small window. A cell. Edmund could recognise them now. 'Stand back from the door!' the sergeant called to someone inside. He slid back a bolt, and jerked his head for Edmund to enter.

A figure sat on the bottom bunk. As Edmund entered, the man rose and stared. 'Well, who have we here?' grinned Archie.

They sailed a few hours later. They heard the *Primrose Bay*'s engines begin to throb, distant orders shouted, the rattle of gangways being drawn up. A deep horn blared, the floor of their cabin trembled, and they felt the ship ease forward. They couldn't see anything. There was just one tiny porthole window in their cabin, high up and sealed shut. Water slapped and chopped against it. We're right down at the waterline, Edmund realised.

'Sounds like I ended up in the same army office as you,' said Archie. 'They told me to put on a uniform, too. When I refused, the officer demanded "What sort of an example do you think you're setting to younger men, Hooper?"'

Archie grinned. 'I told him: "A good one, I hope. The example of not killing people." And they threw me in a cell. So here we are, Edmund, my lad. Off to see the world.'

For the next few days, however, Archie didn't see much at all. As they reached the open sea, the ship began to roll and dip. They staggered when they stood, held onto the walls of the cramped cell as they moved around. After a couple of hours, Archie was lying down. After another hour, he was throwing up.

74   The older man was sick for three days. Edmund strode backwards and forwards across the cell for exercise, wrote letters in his head the way Archie had told him, ate all his meals and half his friend's – Archie moaned when he was offered food, and threw up again. It was the opposite of Mt Eden; now Edmund was doing the looking-after.

By the fourth day, his cellmate was able to sit up and nibble a little bread. 'Oh, goodness,' Archie sighed. 'A firing squad would have been better than that.'

Early that afternoon, boots marched down the corridor. 'Stand back from the door!' a voice barked. Three soldiers with rifles stood outside. 'All right,' snapped one. 'Up on deck with you.'

Edmund had to help Archie up the steps, since he was still weak from sea-sickness. As they came out into the open, they squinted at the bright sunlight, took deep breaths of the fresh salty air.

Edmund gazed around and caught his breath. They stood on an area of deck with rows of troops all around them. William? Edmund thought again, then realised how unlikely it was. And how unlikely that his elder brother would even look at him.

'Prisoners Hayes and Hooper!' Another major stood in front of them. 'Put on those uniforms.' The officer nodded at two folded piles held by other soldiers.

Archie shook his head. Edmund did the same. The major turned to a line of troops beside him. 'Put the uniforms on them.'

Hands seized them both, held them still. Someone behind Edmund began tugging off his jacket. He stood still for a second with shock, then heaved with all the strength he'd built up in the prison quarry. The man behind went flying. Edmund tore his arms free of those holding them.

Instantly, four rifles were aimed at him. Everyone went still. The major's mouth was open. The soldier Edmund had flung off lay sprawled on the deck.

Then heads turned in amazement as Archie laughed. 'Don't shoot us, lads! We're not your enemy. We fight against war.' The major began to speak, but Edmund's friend ignored him. 'We'll take our own clothes off.' He nodded to Edmund. 'More important struggles ahead, my boy.'

When they stood there in their underwear, the army uniforms were put on them. 'Sorry, chum,' a voice breathed in Edmund's ear, as a soldier pulled the khaki tunic down over his head. 'Not my idea.'

Then they were made to sit on wooden boxes, still with the rows of troops watching, and a man gave each of them a haircut, snipping and chopping until all that remained was a bristly stubble. He was rough, shoved their heads from side to side, nicked them with the scissors until blood trickled down their necks.

The rows of troops had stood silently, but now voices began to call. 'That'll show you what blood is, conchie!' 'Going to faint, you cowards?' The major barked 'Silence!'

Their haircuts finished, they were taken back towards the stairs. Edmund gazed at the bright green sea, took more breaths of air.

Without warning, a soldier lunged forward from the ranks, seized him by the collar with one hand, snatched at his tunic with the other. 'Showed you, didn't it? Showed you!'

'Step back!' yapped the major. 'Back to your place!' The soldier moved away, eyes fixed on Edmund. The escort led them below.

'You all right?' Archie sighed, when they were back in their cell and he'd collapsed exhausted onto his bunk. 'Don't be upset by that bloke who grabbed you. They don't always mean it.'

'Oh, he meant it, all right.' Edmund held something out to his friend. Something he'd just taken from his tunic pocket where a hand had thrust it three minutes before. A bar of chocolate.

The days passed. One week ... two ... three. Their main problem now was boredom. They saw only the walls of their cell, heard only the distant noises of the ship and the boots of the men who brought their meals. They walked. Three strides between the walls, over and over until they'd counted to a thousand. But Edmund could feel his body losing its fitness, while Archie looked tired and pale.

Their minds were becoming less fit, too. Three times they asked for something to read, but nothing happened. A couple of hours after their third request, the door of their cell swung open. A soldier slung a small pamphlet on the floor. 'There. Great reading for a conchie.'

Edmund picked it up. *Army Training Manual No. 29. Instructions for Firing and Maintenance of the Lewis Light Machine-Gun.* He was about to hand it back to the soldier when Archie took it from him.

'Thanks. We'll enjoy this.' The man gaped, muttered something, strode out. Edmund's friend grinned at him. 'Better than nothing. And we might as well know what we're up against.'

So they read to each other how to change the drum of ammunition on the Lewis Gun, how to clean the barrel, how to adjust the sight for different distances. They learned bits off by heart and quizzed each other.

They made up their own training manuals. '*Number 42: Instructions for Use of the Light Potato Peeler,*' said Archie. '*Number 178: Instructions for Use of the Heavy Feather Duster,*' said Edmund.

When the same soldier opened their cell door three days later, Edmund smiled and handed him the manual. 'Any more, friend?'

The man glared. 'Don't be cheeky!' But that evening two old history books arrived in their cell. Nobody seemed to know from where.

More days. Another week. Another fortnight. They finished the history books. They recited any poetry they could remember to each other. ('I wandered lonely as a cloud,' went Archie. 'Humpty Dumpty sat on a wall,' went Edmund.) They talked about their lives.

'My older brother has enlisted,' Edmund said. 'He told me that what I'm doing is stupid and cowardly. We haven't—' he heard his voice start to shake '—we haven't spoken to each other for over a year.'

Archie nodded. 'My sister is the same. When I said I wouldn't serve in the Army, she swore she'd never speak to me again. Her daughters – my nieces – they're five and seven years old. Their mother told them I'm evil, and they must never come near me.' He shook his head.

They were taken up on deck again. No haircut this time. They stood in their unwanted uniforms while troops did bayonet practice, thrusting the long blades into bundles of cloth, with wild yells. Edmund imagined the steel stabbing into live bodies and shuddered.

No sign of William. Why should he be on this ship, anyway? Edmund thought. He may already be in France. Or he may not have left New Zealand. Around them, the sea was a choppy dark blue. The air was colder. They must be getting near England, surely.

That night, as they sat and talked in their cell, bells rang far below. Voices shouted, feet hurried up metal ladders. The *Primrose Bay* turned, sharply enough to make them clutch the sides of their bunks, and the engines picked up speed.

The cell door flew open. Two soldiers stared at them. 'There's been a submarine alert. If anything happens, follow us up on deck. Don't try and escape, or we'll shoot.'

Edmund couldn't help smiling. 'Escape? We're not fish.'

An hour later, the engines reduced speed again. The cell door was locked and the soldiers left. Archie nodded to Edmund. 'They still don't know what to do with us.'

Another five days. More boots, more door-opening, and the major who'd ordered their haircuts stepped into the cell. Archie smiled, said 'Good morning', and stretched out a hand. The major automatically took it to shake, then snatched his away.

'This is your last chance to show some honour and loyalty. When we land, I have no control over what is done to you. Are you willing to do your duty and serve your King and Country?'

Archie smiled again. 'No, thank you.' Edmund swallowed, then shook his head. The officer glared at them. 'Then you have only yourselves to blame for what happens next. I wash my hands of you.'

He stamped out. Archie smiled a third time – at Edmund. 'A Roman governor also washed his hands when he gave Christ over to be crucified. Bear up, my lad. We'll be strong.'

Edmund hadn't been able to prevent a shiver of fear at the officer's words. But now he relaxed again. With Archie beside him, he could face anything.

Two days later, they landed in England and were separated.

DEAR Mother,

I AM well.

I HAVE BEEN training.

I WILL WRITE again soon.

I HAVE BEEN on the ship to England.

I WOULD LIKE a letter, at any time.

My dear Mother, we're only allowed to fill in an army message card. I don't know if they'll cross out this bit, but I'll write it anyway. We have arrived in England, and now I can really begin to play my part. Don't worry about me. My love to you and Jessie.

Your Loving Son

William

William

William sailed from the same wharf where Edmund had been taken. But it was a different ship and a very different departure.

They marched through the streets with their commanding officer riding on a horse in front of them. There were banners reading

WE'RE PROUD OF YOU

and

SONS OF THE EMPIRE.

Bands played. Crowds of people cheered and waved, although William glimpsed a few women weeping or watching silently. Small boys ran along beside them. Girls tossed flowers and blew kisses. A couple of them called 'Good luck, Ginger!' to Jerry, whose face blushed as red as his hair.

They waited beside the loading sheds, staring up at the tall steel sides of the *Empire Star*. 'She used to be a passenger liner,' someone in William's No. 3 Platoon said. 'Reckon we'll get breakfast in bed?'

Another voice went, 'There's a bunch of conchies being shipped over to the trenches. Let's tip them into the sea first.'

A third soldier, further along the line, said, 'No, they were on the other boat, the one that sailed a few days back.'

William felt relieved. If he came face to face with his younger brother, he didn't know what he'd say. Anyway, that wasn't likely to happen. A few conchies might be taken to Europe, but Edmund was probably in a work camp or a cell, somewhere in New Zealand.

It took over three hours for them all to get on board. The officers were in the First Class cabins; the other ranks were crammed into Second and Third Class, some in cabins, some on the floor of the ballroom, the library or the games room. Moving along a corridor meant squeezing past blokes sitting on their kitbags, waiting for a place to call their own.

They sailed that evening. It was a sight William knew he would never forget. Hundreds – no, *thousands* – of troops, standing at the rails, crowding the outside steps up to the next deck, even clinging to the ladders on the sides of funnels. All of them waving their hats and cheering. The crowd filling the wharf below, a mass of upturned faces, waving back, cheering also or crying. Bands on board and on shore, playing 'It's a Long Way to Tipperary' and 'Wish Me Luck As You Wave Me Goodbye'.

The thin strip of water between ship and wharf churned into foam as the engines began to turn, and grew wider until the streamers held by hands on deck and on shore tightened and snapped. The wharves and buildings shrank behind, and the troops fell silent, until the only sounds were the throb of engines and the cries of seabirds wheeling overhead.

By next morning, there was no sign of land. The ship began to dip and rise as it met the waves of the open sea. Some men became quiet, turned green and rushed for the rails as their stomachs also dipped and rose.

William met a pale-faced Herbert coming shakily back down the stairs to their cabin. His face looked different. 'Losht my falsh teef,' he mumbled. 'They fell into the shea while I wash being shick. I—' Herbert paused, gulped, then turned and fled up the stairs and out onto the deck again.

William meanwhile had never felt so well in his life. He stood at the stern, watching the white tumble of wake spread behind them and the distant flat line of the horizon on all sides. This was an adventure, all right. Now things had really begun.

After four days, when most of the seasick men were recovering, they began training again. Physical drill, kit inspection, bayonet training, signalling with flags. Every part of every deck was packed with lines of men and shouting NCOs. They even had rifle practice, shooting at a big wooden box towed a hundred yards behind the ship.

In the late afternoons and evenings, there were tug-of-war contests on deck between different platoons, quizzes and singalongs, lectures from officers about Great Britain or France. William learned to say '*Bonjour* . . . Hello. *Merci* . . . Thank you', and felt pleased. Jerry learned to say '*Bonjour, jolie fille* . . . Hello, pretty girl', and looked *very* pleased.

'Some ships have their own cinema!' one soldier claimed. 'You can watch films on board.'

The others laughed and went 'Never!' But the first soldier insisted. 'And the Americans are inventing a way of people talking on films.' This time everyone laughed and went '*Absolutely* never!'

Three weeks slid by. The *Empire Star* ploughed steadily through the water. It was hard for William to believe there was a war on. Hard until he saw the lookouts during the daytime, standing on the highest decks, watching in all directions with binoculars in case any strange ships appeared on the horizon. Until he noticed how at night, every outside light was turned off so the ship sailed on in total darkness.

One morning at the end of the third week, land lay ahead, low and shimmering in the sun. South Africa. They steamed into port, pushing slowly through swarms of small boats, on which dark-skinned men held up fruit, wooden carvings, even live monkeys, shouting to the soldiers to throw down money.

They spent just one day in the port of Cape Town, taking on oil and food. They were allowed five hours' shore leave, and William walked into town with his friends, blinking in the hot sun. People stared at them as they went past. 'People must think we're really handsome,' Jack grinned. Then William heard a voice sneer 'Who's your black pal?', and began to understand.

They went into a restaurant and tried to order a meal. But the Indian manager said 'No. No, sorry'. He pointed at Jack Kahui. 'People make trouble if I serve him. Please go. So sorry.'

'What was all that about?' asked Jack, as they stood outside. Then they saw the group of young white men glaring at them and especially at Jack. William called out, 'What are you blokes looking so unhappy about? Is it the end of the world if we're friends with someone who's a different colour?'

'My elder cousin fought against this lot in the Boer War, just fifteen years ago,' grunted Herbert, as they walked on. 'Now we're supposed to be on their side, but it looks like some of them are ready to fight us again.'

On they sailed, into a storm that sent the big liner lurching from side to side, and also sent men staggering across decks, thudding into rails, skidding off-balance and nearly falling down stairways.

One young soldier did fall, flung down a ladder as the ship plunged into a trough between two huge waves. He smashed head-first into a steel bulkhead, and died two days later.

His funeral was held on a morning when the ocean lay still and glittering. The storm was gone. Bells rang, and the ship's engines stopped. The body lay wrapped in a sheet, under a New Zealand flag, while rows of troops stood silently. 'Atten-*shun*!' a sergeant-major shouted, and hundreds of pairs of boots crashed together. 'Hats off!'

An army padre read the service. A trumpeter played 'The Last Post', its notes fading across the sea where two grey birds glided and called. The stretcher was tilted, and the white-shrouded body slid from under the flag, to disappear beneath the surface. Total silence for a few seconds, then Jack began to sing quietly in Maori. Other voices joined in, and William felt a shiver run down his spine. Another moment he'd never forget.

They crossed the Equator. Two weeks since South Africa. Three. The daytime training went on. Officers told them in lectures how the Germans were dropping bombs on London from their huge Zeppelin airships, but British fighter planes were shooting many of them down. The United States was sure to enter the war on Great Britain's side. New weapons to fight the Hun were being invented, and it could only be a matter of months before Germany surrendered. 'We heard better rumours in camp,' Herbert whispered. Meanwhile, a couple of NCOs who'd fought in the first years of the war muttered and shook their heads.

The days grew cooler, the sky duller. Europe was getting closer. White clouds lay along the horizon. More seabirds appeared, curving over the ship, fighting for the rubbish tipped from the stern.

A Thursday morning. Nearly seven weeks since they'd left home. They were on deck, starting a session of physical drill, when one of the lookouts shouted. 'Ships!'

They came sweeping towards the *Empire Star*. Four of them, small and grey and dangerous-looking. 'They're British!' another voice called. Yes, William realised. They had to be, since the liner kept its course, sailing steadily towards them. After five minutes, he could see the white ensigns of the Royal Navy streaming from their masts.

Uniformed sailors stood on their decks, waving. The troops waved back and cheered. Deep blasts from the liner's horn; answering blasts from the four newcomers. 'Destroyers,' someone said. 'Come to see us safely into port, in case there are any Hun submarines around.'

The grey shapes wheeled, white water curving from their bows, and took up positions on either side of the liner. William could see the guns on their decks, long and dark and lethal.

The cloud on the horizon was grey this time. No, not a cloud. Land. Slowly it took shape. Hills and valleys. Trees and farms. Houses. A town – a big town, with wharves and cranes and bustling tugboats.

Jerry stood beside William at the rail. 'Is it London?' he asked eagerly.

'No, Portsmouth,' said one voice.

'No, Bristol,' said a second.

'No, Dover,' said a third.

'Wait and you'll find out,' said Sergeant Molloy.

Tugboats eased them towards a grimy wharf. The men waiting there with ropes looked small and tough. They didn't wave or smile.

'Look!' went another voice from 3 Platoon. 'Over there.'

William and the others stared at where the man was pointing. A warship, up against another wharf. A bigger one than the destroyers: a cruiser perhaps? One funnel shattered and hanging over the side. Great holes torn in the other funnel and all along the hull. Smashed gun turrets with gun barrels pointing crookedly at the sky. The bows half ripped away. Black stains where fire must have swept through the ship. Everyone stared in silence. The war wasn't far away.

PART 4

GETTING READY

Dearest Ma,

Here's another letter that may never reach you. I'm in an army camp in England. I don't know exactly where. We travelled here through beautiful countryside – farms, cottages with thatched roofs, white horses pulling a hay wagon. It's hard to believe England is at war.

I don't know where Archie is, either. Or if there are any other people like me in the camp. The Army likes to keep things secret! Several officers have tried to make me change my mind, but I feel more determined than ever.

There are wounded soldiers here, working in the kitchens and gardens. Some of them have lost an arm or a leg. Some look as if they have seen dreadful things. I keep thinking: Why should young men have their lives ruined like this? I think of William, too. Please send him my kind wishes. I don't want this bitterness between us to last.

Dear Ma, I may not see you for a long time. My love to you and Jessie always. I don't know what may happen to me, but I'll never regret what I've decided to do.

Your Loving Son

Edmund

Edmund

In fact, Edmund *did* have some idea of what might happen to him.

Soldiers – those who hated him because he was a CO – had told him. 'They'll take you to France, march you up to the trenches and stand you out in front so the Huns can have target practice,' said one. 'They'll sentence you to death by firing squad,' went another. 'They'll lock you in a cell and let you starve like the rubbish you are,' sneered a third.

Yet it wasn't easy to believe in trenches or death, with the peaceful English countryside around. Beyond the high wire fences circling the camp were farms with new green wheat or black-and-white cows like those at home. On a low ridge a mile or so away, the grey bulk of an ancient castle stood against the sky.

The camp itself wasn't pretty. It was rows of big round tents in which the troops slept, plus bare wooden buildings going up as fast as carpenters could build them. The ground had been churned to mud by thousands of boots. Lines of rough boards, nailed together in five-foot lengths ('duckboards', Edmund learned they were called) provided pathways that slowly sank into the ground as feet tramped across them. Inside the camp, there were no trees or shrubs. No grass. Just tents, raw new buildings, weapons and thousands of men training.

As he was marched in for the first time by yet another escort, rows of troops were at bayonet practice. Stripped to the waist, sweating and yelling, they charged and stabbed at straw dummies strapped to posts. 'Should put you there, conchie,' grunted the corporal leading him. 'If you've got enough guts to make a target.'

He was brought before another officer, a tall elderly man with a crown and two pips on his shoulder tabs. 'I'm Colonel Brabin,' the man told him, pleasantly enough. 'As Camp Commandant, it's my duty to see you are treated fairly. But I must tell you that you'll find life here far more pleasant if you give up this nonsense now and agree to serve your King and Country.'

It was the same approach that Edmund had met before. He replied politely. ('Always show good manners,' Archie had told him. 'We want people to see we're civilised as well as stubborn.') 'I'm sorry,' he said. 'I can't accept orders to kill other people.'

94

The colonel watched him. 'But you're the only person here who feels that way. What good can you do?'

This wasn't hard. 'There are many who think like me. But even if I *was* the only one, that wouldn't make my feelings any less genuine.'

Colonel Brabin tapped his pen on the table in front of him. 'Don't you have any loyalty to the British

Empire, man?'

Edmund had already heard this argument, too. 'Yes, I do. But that's no reason to kill other humans, just because they come from a country we don't agree with.'

'So what would you do if you saw a German soldier attacking your mother or your sister? Stand by and watch?'

Edmund almost smiled. He and Archie had talked about this very question. 'No, I would try and stop him – with as little violence as possible. But what has that got to do with war and being told to murder young men who have never done me any harm?'

The colonel's neck began to turn red. '*I'm* asking the questions, Hayes!' He was silent briefly, then: 'Surely you can serve as a stretcher-bearer. Then you won't be taking lives. You'll be helping save them.'

Edmund felt tired suddenly. Always the same questions. Wouldn't people ever listen to him? Perhaps the cause he and Archie believed in was hopeless after all?

He made himself stand taller. This was exactly what the Army wanted him to feel. 'Of course, if a person was injured, I'd want to help. That's simply common kindness. It has nothing to do with war.'

'Don't start giving me lectures! The Army has been more than reasonable with you. If you persist in your stupidity, you'll be sent to the battlefront.'

A chill touched Edmund's back, but he tried to keep his voice calm. 'I will still hold to my views.' He remembered Archie's advice. 'Thank you for listening to me.'

The colonel didn't seem to know what to say. He flicked his hand at the escort. 'Take him away.'

The cell was much the same as other cells, although made of wood instead of stone. Bare walls, a door with a grille, one window too high to see through, no furniture except for a toilet bucket in one corner.

But it was so cold. A bitter grey wind seemed to blow endlessly across the camp. It whined through gaps in the hastily built walls, chilling Edmund to his bones. He had no blanket until evening, when a thin grey one was tossed into his cell. Until then, he paced up and down, slapping his arms across his body, stamping his feet in their badly fitting army boots, blowing into his cupped hands in a vain attempt to get warm. He tried to count as he walked, the way he had on ship. 'One . . . two . . . three . . .' But he was shivering too much to speak the words.

There was no mattress, and on the cold floor it was hours before he slept. The thin blanket hardly helped at all. He was still huddled miserably on the floor, half-aware that the square of high window had changed from black to dull grey, when the door crashed open, and the corporal who had talked about using him for bayonet practice stamped in, two other soldiers behind him. 'On your feet, conchie! Report for drill!'

Edmund struggled up, body shuddering with cold. 'I can . . . not,' his teeth were chattering, and it was hard to form the words, '. . . not obey any military order.'

Next minute he was sprawling on the floor again. The corporal had kicked his legs from under him. His head hurt, where it had struck against the wall. The man glared down at him. 'Report for drill, I said.'

Edmund managed to shake his head. 'No. I—' He saw the NCO draw back his boot and knew another kick was coming. He tried to hunch up, to protect himself.

A voice said something, and other boots stepped forward. One of the soldiers gripped the corporal's arm, pulled him back. The NCO spun around and snatched his arm free. He stared at the soldier, down at Edmund, then strode from the cell.

The soldier spoke to Edmund. 'Get up if you can, chum. Corporal McKean says we've got to take you around the camp, so the lads can see you. Better to walk than be dragged.'

Edmund hauled himself up. The corporal was out in the corridor, angry-faced. 'March him right around. Let them see what a coward looks like. Put the cuffs on him!'

For a moment, Edmund tried to decide whether to let his arms go limp, so the soldiers had to seize them for the handcuffs. But there was no point in just making their job harder. He held out his hands, and the steel bracelets were snapped on. He noticed that the soldier had been careful not to make them painfully tight.

For two hours, he was marched around the muddy paths and across the drill squares of the camp. Rather, his escort marched. Edmund walked. Yet again, he kept his head up as he went, met the gaze of the soldiers they passed. They looked puzzled. Some frowned, but he got a few nods that were almost sympathetic. He was glad of the exercise; it put some warmth into his body.

The next three mornings, he was taken out again and marched around. By the fourth morning, several soldiers were greeting him. One walked up, ignoring the escort, and put some biscuits into Edmund's cuffed hands.

But the cell was hard to endure. He was locked in all afternoon and night, and he'd never been so cold in his life. The lukewarm food didn't help. By the morning of the fifth day, his throat was sore, and his forehead felt hot.

His escort had begun putting the cuffs on him, as usual. Corporal McKean, who had waited out in the corridor on previous mornings, stalked in and glared.

'Tighter!'

One of the other soldiers began to speak. Then they all sprang to attention as another figure appeared in the doorway. A captain.

The newcomer stepped into the cell. He glanced at where Edmund's single blanket lay waiting to be taken away. 'Is this prisoner on special punishment?'

'No, sir,' said the corporal. 'But—'

'Then give him another blanket. What's the point of having another sick man to deal with?'

The captain left. Corporal McKean gave Edmund a glare. But that night, two blankets were tossed into his cell.

He was getting weaker. He didn't have the work and exercise he'd had in the prison quarry back in New Zealand. The freezing cell, poor food and uncertainty about what would happen were all wearing him down. He'd felt himself losing strength on the ship. Now, alone and locked away for long hours out of the daylight, with a heavy cold that kept him wheezing and coughing, he knew his health was fading.

Three days later, the pair of soldiers in charge of Edmund took him as usual past the parade grounds where lines of troops did physical training or rifle drill. But instead of carrying along inside the wire fences of the camp, they marched him out the front gate and into the countryside.

At first, Edmund wondered if he was being taken to another camp, or even on the first stages of a journey to France and the battlefields. But after half a mile, the three of them reached a lane leading off between rows of green trees. They followed the lane for another hundred yards, then turned off and walked around to the back of a stone-walled barn.

'Sit yourself down,' one of the soldiers told Edmund. 'You look like you could do with some fresh air.'

The sudden kindness, plus the sight of gentle fields of wheat stretching away to soft green hedges, was almost too much for Edmund. He managed to murmur thanks, then he sat with his back against the barn wall, already warm from the sun, and took deep, slow breaths. Bees hummed among the wildflowers beside him. A bird trilled in the high blue air.

100

The soldiers sat beside him. One offered a cigarette. Edmund shook his head. 'No, thanks.' For a few minutes, the three sat in silence. A wagon or something rumbled along a road in the distance.

'Why are you doing this, pal?' the soldier who'd led them down the lane finally asked. 'You're giving yourself a rough time.'

It was harder to explain to these quiet listeners than to the officers and others he'd faced. Edmund tried. 'I'm opposed to all killing . . . wars only make things worse.'

The other soldier nodded. 'I joined up because my missus needs the money. There's little work where I come from. Plus someone sent a pal of mine a white feather in the post because he hadn't enlisted. That says you're a coward. So I joined up before they did the same to me.'

The first soldier's voice was tight. 'The Huns killed my older brother. In the first year of the war. A machine-gun got him. I joined because I want to kill some of them. I don't hate you, chum. It's Germans I hate.'

They were quiet again. Edmund thought of his own older brother. The wagon rumbled on. It didn't seem to be any nearer or further away. Then the first soldier spoke again. 'Hear the guns?'

As Edmund stared, the soldier continued, 'It's the artillery. Thousands of them, they reckon, all firing at once. No wonder you can hear them all the way from France.'

101

More days passed. Even with the extra blanket, Edmund's cell was almost unbearably cold. He coughed most of the time now. A couple of mornings as they marched him around the camp, he had to ask his escort to stop.

'I need . . . to breathe,' he wheezed. The soldiers who'd taken him out into the country had been replaced by others. Edmund hoped the first two hadn't got into trouble.

He worried about William. The artillery rumbling – fifty? eighty? – miles away showed how huge this war must be. He worried about Archie as well. Where was he? How was the older man's health standing up to things? As he was taken past the cookhouse one morning, Edmund glimpsed a thin, pale figure reflected in a window, trudging between two soldiers. His stomach lurched as he realised it was himself.

Doubts began to nag at him. He knew from what he'd heard that troops in the trenches were suffering far more, but how much longer could he endure this empty, pointless life? Should he agree to be a stretcher-bearer, or offer to work in the camp garden? 'No!' He jerked as he heard himself speak out loud again. Both of those would be supporting the Army, and he'd never do that.

Only two things happened in the weeks that followed. First, the United States declared war on Germany, after a German submarine sank an American passenger liner. The soldiers were delighted. 'Millions of new blokes on our side. The Hun has signed his own death warrant.'

Perhaps the war will end faster now, Edmund thought. Perhaps William will be safer.

Three days after that, as he was being marched past

the cookhouse again, a man in civilian clothes came out, heading for a wagon piled with cabbages and onions. Edmund glanced at him, then stared.

The left side of the young man's face was one huge scar, a twisted ridge of white-blue flesh from mouth to ear. In fact, there was no ear on that side, just more scar tissue. No eye, either: only a raw slit between two folds of skin.

'Got hit by a piece of shell two years back,' one of his escorts muttered as they moved on. 'Poor lad.'

Then one grey, drizzly afternoon, everything changed. Edmund had come back damp and cold from the morning march. His half-dish of lukewarm soup and piece of tough bread put no warmth into him. Nor did his walking backwards and forwards between the walls.

Boots tramped down the corridor. 'Stand back from the door!' The cell door clashed open, and Corporal McKean stood there.

'I've got news for you, Hayes. They're taking you to France tomorrow. You'll be dead inside a week.'

My Dear Mother,

I'm allowed to send you a proper letter this time, not just a postcard. However, there are lots of things we're not supposed to write down. They say German spies are everywhere.

But I can tell you that we've been in a training camp in England for the last month. It's been hard. It's been boring. But it's made better soldiers of us. If I was back in Mr Parkinson's factory now, I could run everywhere!

I can't wait to be where things are really happening, and give the Hun what he deserves. He's already been hit hard and he can't last much longer. I just hope the war isn't over before I have the chance to do my bit. The other blokes all feel the same way.

The camp here is surrounded by farms. The buildings are so old. One English chap I talked to lives in a house built three hundred years ago. Can you imagine that?

I've been to London! We had a forty-eight-hour leave, and so a lot of us caught a train there. You won't believe how big it is. I saw the Tower of London. I saw fire engines with women crews! We were going to pop in and say hello to the King, but he was busy.

Dear Mother, it may not be easy for me to send a letter when I'm finally in the trenches. But I will keep thinking of you and dear Jessie. I send my love to you both. Is there any news of Edmund?

Your Loving Son

William

William

The words about Edmund were down on the paper almost before he realised. He stared at them, lifted his pen to cross them out, left them as they were.

He looked at what he'd written. He hadn't mentioned the big old tents that rain leaked through and wind blew through. He'd mentioned the farms, but not the route marches that took the troops past them day after day. A lot of the farm workers were women and girls; many of their men were off fighting. They watched the New Zealanders march past, but seldom smiled or waved.

'Used to be all cheers and blowing kisses at the start of the war,' an English NCO told William. 'Too many deaths since then. And the Army took away half their horses, to pull guns and wagons.'

They took their turn on sentry duty, standing with rifle and bayonet at the front gates to the camp. 'If ten thousand Germans attack down this road, you shout "Halt!" and we'll capture them while they're standing still,' Sergeant Molloy told William and Herbert.

They did Physical Training, stretching and bending in rows, while an NCO on a wooden platform shouted orders through a megaphone.

They practised scaling walls, lifting a man up as

he stood on a rifle held between two of them, then dragging themselves up as he stretched another rifle down to them.

They dug yards of trenches, grumbling all the time, learning how to strengthen the walls with timber, so heavy rain or shell-bursts wouldn't make them collapse. 'We won't just be – gardeners after the war,' panted Jerry. 'We'll be – miners, too.'

Jack patted him on the shoulder. 'And we can use your hair to light up the tunnels.'

They learned also how a length of trench should be a zigzag shape, not a straight line, to give protection from any shells landing in them, or from any enemy who managed to capture part of the trench.

As the weeks passed, William got to know the other soldiers of 3 Platoon even better. Quick-tempered Jerry, who rushed into everything and who never stopped asking when they'd see some real fighting and give the Hun a shock. Strong, smiling Jack. Herbert, older than the rest of them, quiet and thoughtful.

He got to know the platoon NCO and officer, too. Sergeant Molloy was a blacksmith who had fought in South Africa's Boer War. Mr Gowing, the lieutenant, had been a doctor before this war and was younger than half the men he commanded.

English officers ran the training camp. Since most of the younger ones were over in France, these were often retired men who had volunteered to help when war broke out. One was so fat that it took two soldiers to lift him up onto his horse. Another instructed them in marching drill while sitting in a wheelchair.

They sat on more hard wooden forms while a major told them that the British Empire, France, the United States, Russia, Belgium, Italy, Japan and Romania were all good because they were on our side, while Germany, Austria-Hungary, Turkey and Bulgaria were all bad because they were the enemy. 'Hope he didn't mix any of 'em up,' whispered a voice, and William didn't know whether to grin or feel shocked.

A captain told them how Germany and its allies were running out of food and men and weapons, and one good battle would finish them. A colonel told them that the British were pushing forward everywhere in France and Belgium. Their own Mr Gowing, looking nervous, gave them a lecture on machine-guns. When he finished, some of 3 Platoon began to clap, until the NCOs shouted 'Silence!'

They scrubbed their clothes in cold water with hard yellow soap. They had kit inspections every morning: if a single folded blanket was half an inch crooked, or a single bootlace unwashed, they had to run around the parade ground five times with their rifles held over their heads.

They were weighed and given a medical examination.

Their teeth were checked, and Herbert got new false ones. 'I'm going to get six fillings!' Jerry said excitedly. 'For nothing!' Never before had William met anyone who rushed into the dentist's chair.

Every day there was rifle practice. 'Twelve aimed shots in one minute!' the corporal instructing them yelled. 'That's what you have to do. A platoon of thirty rifles should sound like three machine-guns firing!' Their new targets were shaped like charging soldiers with snarling faces.

They threw more Mills Bombs. They did more bayonet practice. They laid telephone wires along the sides of trenches and in narrow slits across the open ground to help with communications. They built hidden observation posts up trees. 'Pretend you're a sparrow,' Sergeant Molloy told them. Herbert grinned. 'Never seen a sparrow wearing a helmet, Sarge.'

They learned First Aid: how to bandage wounds; how two of them could make a seat with clasped hands for a wounded man to sit on while they carried him. When William and Herbert tried to carry Jerry that way, their hands slipped apart, and their friend fell in the mud.

109

Sergeant Molloy shook his head. 'If I get wounded on the battlefield, please leave me there to die.' He stared at Jerry, who was brushing mud off the seat of his trousers. 'And you, you horrible little man, you've got a dirty bottom!'

But they didn't laugh at other First Aid training. Especially the photographs of young men with stumps instead of legs, or a hand with only one finger and a thumb left. 'They look bad,' Mr Gowing told his silent platoon, 'but First Aid saved their lives. So pay attention!'

After three weeks, their training grew more complicated. On a flat field a mile from camp, they practised more attacks, advancing in rushes through gaps in their own barbed wire, then spreading out into lines and striding forward while another imaginary artillery barrage kept moving ahead of them, and real machine-gun bullets whipped overhead.

They marched further from camp, to a dry plain dotted with boulders, and watched as teams of horses and a tractor pulled six big guns into a line. 'Howitzers,' a voice said. 'Medium artillery.' Then they practised moving forward behind a real barrage, fire and smoke and earth hurtling upwards in a wall of noise just fifty yards in front of them. William realised he was gripping his rifle so hard, his wrists ached. His ears hummed with the explosions. Smoke stung his eyes.

A flying clod of earth sped past Jerry, and the red-headed soldier flung himself on the ground. 'Get up!' yelled Sergeant Molloy. 'That's friendly dirt!'

When the guns finally stopped firing, they stared at one another, shocked and excited.

It wasn't all training. They had rest times, when they lay on their beds and played cards or talked. Herbert hoped to get married when he returned to New Zealand, he told them. His fiancée was a nurse, whom he'd met in the church choir. William didn't say anything, but he kept thinking of dark-haired Violet.

One afternoon, 3 Platoon played cricket against 1 Platoon, thirty-a-side. There was cheering and laughing. William tried to imagine these same men shooting to kill others. The game made him think of his younger, sport-loving brother. Where was he now? How had they grown so far apart? It was Edmund's fault.

They were given two days' leave in London, and William thought Jerry would burst with excitement. A troop train took them through miles of suburbs, until dark tall buildings rose ahead. Huge balloons like giant grey cylinders floated over the city, tied to long wire cables. They were there to stop German bombers, but William knew that the enemy's great Zeppelin airships had flown above them and attacked factories.

He didn't know what to think of London. There were

more people in one big shop than in his whole town back home. Everyone was in a hurry; hardly anyone smiled. He and Jack, Herbert and Jerry ate in a restaurant and couldn't believe how expensive things were. 'Someone's making money out of this war,' Jack muttered.

When they came out, a young man in a suit was standing on the footpath nearby, gazing blankly across the road. A woman passing by stopped, then spoke to him. 'Why haven't you joined up? Why aren't you fighting?'

The young man took no notice of her and kept staring into space. The woman got angry. 'Are you too frightened? Here's something for you!' From her handbag, she pulled out something white. William glimpsed a feather. The sign of a coward.

The woman shoved the feather into the young man's hand, and he jerked as if he'd been hit. At the same moment, an older woman came rushing out of the next-door shop. 'Leave my son alone! You stupid fool! He was blinded in a German gas attack. Oh, you stupid, ignorant fool!'

112

The woman with the feather hurried off. The older woman burst into tears. The young man reached out uncertainly until he touched her, then put his arms around her. William and his friends moved silently away.

Not everyone returned to camp after the London leave. Two men from another platoon were missing. One turned up drunk the next day and was put in a cell. There was no sign of the other.

'Deserted,' voices said. 'Run away and trying to hide somewhere. They'll shoot the fool if he doesn't give himself up.'

Conscientious objectors were in another camp near-by, other voices claimed. A few men, Jerry included, announced how they'd like to stick a uniform on them and shove a rifle into their cowardly hands. Herbert shook his head. 'They've got their own courage.' William said nothing. Might Edmund . . . No, he probably wasn't even in England. And if he was, William had nothing to say to him.

The next day, on a route march, they passed a field with two rows of old tents and a barbed-wire fence going up all around. There were soldiers with rifles, and fifty or so men in grey uniforms, standing or sitting in small groups.

'They're Huns!' someone said. 'Prisoners!' Everyone stared at the strangers, who stared back. Some of them looked frightened. They edged away from the road and the marching troops. There were arms in slings, bandaged heads, men on crutches. A couple of them seemed only seventeen or eighteen. Others were as old as Mr Parkinson from the factory. None of them looked savage; just tired and lost.

Things were changing in the camp. Rumours sped backwards and forwards again. 'The Hun trenches in France are ten feet deep, with concrete walls and platforms for machine-guns. Nothing can destroy them' . . . 'Both sides are digging enormous tunnels to reach under the other's trenches' . . . 'Yes, and they're packing them with explosives to blow the enemy sky-high.' As usual, nobody knew what to believe.

More frighteningly, they were shown how to put on gas-masks and then had to walk through a long building full of yellow-white smoke. Nobody knew if it was real gas.

'Don't run!' NCOs ordered them as they went in. 'Learn what it's like!'

William's mouth felt dry. Under the sour-smelling mask, his face streamed with sweat. Through the goggles, he glimpsed figures stumbling forward through the smoke. Someone was gasping, almost sobbing.

When he blundered out into the wonderful fresh air and yanked the mask from his face, he heard yelling down at the far end where they'd entered. A soldier he didn't recognise was wrenching his mask off, shouting 'No! I won't! No!' Two NCOs were pulling him away.

They spent a whole morning cleaning boots, rifles, bayonets, belts, uniforms, even their lemon-squeezer hats. Then they marched past a wooden stand, where a fierce-looking officer with a white moustache and red tabs on his collar stood, saluting stiffly. 'A general,' someone said.

'Hope we don't have to do many more of these,' Jerry grumbled when the parade was over. 'I didn't join the bloomin' Army to polish boots.'

They didn't have to do *any* more parades. Two days later, they left for France.

PART 5

THE
TRENCHES

DEAR Mother and Jessie

I AM well.

I HAVE BEEN in camp.

I WILL WRITE again, as soon as I can.

I WOULD LIKE some warm socks!

YOUR Loving Son,

William

William

There were so many things he wanted to write, but wasn't allowed to.

LOOSE LIPS SINK SHIPS!

read a poster urging everyone to be careful what they said. 'A Silly Letter Does It Better,' said Jack, but nobody laughed.

I want to say how much I miss you, William told his mother and sister inside his head. How I feel excited but scared at what's about to happen to me. How I'd love to hear all about home, and Jessie's shop, and the tennis club, and . . . and Violet and her other friends – even the ones who giggle all the time. How I want to be with you all, but at the same time I can hardly wait to be in France, whatever happens there.

And I want to ask about Edmund. Was he in that camp near ours? What if we'd met and . . . But William couldn't imagine what would have happened.

When he'd enlisted, everything had seemed so simple. They would get to Europe, thrash the Huns, then return as heroes. Everyone except for a few wrong-headed people like Edmund felt the same way. Now, nothing seemed so clear. Maybe it would in the trenches. William hoped so.

It was William's first time in a really foreign country, where people didn't speak English.

The moment they filed off the ship that had carried them across the English Channel, French voices were all around them. Wharf workers, horse-and-cart drivers, railwaymen. All of them shouting and waving arms and pouring out torrents of words.

William thought of Jerry carefully learning to say 'Hello, pretty girl'. He glanced at the group of grimy, moustached, grunting wharf workers lowering a howitzer onto a wagon just along from where 3 Platoon stood waiting, and chuckled to himself.

They'd done a lot of waiting between England and France. Waiting for the train that took them to the ship – an old ferry boat with machine-guns mounted on its deck. Waiting for the other ferries to fill with troops, and then for the fast, grim-looking destroyers to come steaming up and join them. Waiting in the middle of the Channel, with the destroyers circling them. Nobody knew why they'd stopped, but everyone kept staring at the smooth green water, half-expecting to see the bubbling trail of a torpedo, and those who couldn't swim made sure they stood near the lifeboats.

Finally, there was the waiting to get off the ferries and

onto the trains that took them towards the battlefield. There were times when life in the Army seemed to be all waiting.

'I didn't join the Army just to sit around!' Jerry complained.

'Me, neither,' said Jack. 'I joined to lie down.' And he did, on the hard ground.

At a railway siding near the wharf, an engine with a long line of wagons stood snorting steam. 'Well, men,' said Mr Gowing. 'There's straw on the wagon floors. That's your seats, I'm afraid.'

A few groans. Then someone asked, 'Sir? What's that writing in French on the wagons? With those numbers?'

Their platoon officer gazed at the words. 'It means "Five Horses or Thirty Men". Lucky they haven't mixed you in together.'

Laughter. Then another voice shouted: 'Look! Up there!'

William and the others stared where the man was pointing. Inland, high in the bright blue sky, half a dozen black specks circled and twisted. Birds chasing one another, thought William. Then he saw one of the specks begin to plunge downwards, dark smoke trailing behind it, and he realised. A German plane? A British or French one? They watched and wondered.

In the wagons, they sat uncomfortably on their packs, or on the damp, smelly straw that covered the metal floor.

121

At last, whistles blew, flags waved, a lot more French was shouted, and with a jolt that threw half of them off their packs the train began to move.

Past other trains and more troops they clanked. Past horses being led up ramps into other wagons, tossing their heads and whinnying. Past a square where women in headscarves and black dresses stood talking.

Then they were in open country. They sat or sprawled, dozed or talked or played cards, stared up for any more planes.

But when Herbert called 'Look!' he wasn't pointing at the sky. On a road nearby, two black horses lay beside a shattered cart. The animals were stiff and bloated. William saw with a shock that the back legs of one were missing. A hole half the size of their railway wagon gaped in the road next to the dead animals. Clay and dirt were scattered all around. Another hole had torn up the edge twenty yards further along. Shells, William realised. He and the rest of 3 Platoon watched silently as their train jolted on.

Half an hour later, they all stared out of the open door again. They were passing through a town.

What remained of a town, rather. Piles of smashed bricks lay alongside the road and railway line. Whole walls had fallen or been blown away, so they gazed into the insides of houses. A bed and a wardrobe; a chair and a table. Next minute, it was Jerry who said 'Look!'

and pointed at another wrecked building. Rows of desks: they were looking into a schoolroom. What had happened to the children? Were they inside when the shells hit?

A church was smashed, every piece of glass gone from its arched windows. A big building, with several beds in every room – a hospital, so ruined that they could see right through the collapsed walls and out the other side. Nothing moved on the streets except for a few skinny dogs.

It was mid-afternoon when the train finally stopped. William and the rest of 3 Platoon climbed down and formed up. A few hundred yards away, across bare fields, lay yet another army camp, with its high wire fences and rows of big tents. This time, though, there was something different. Spaced along the fences, steel barrels pointed towards the sky. Anti-aircraft guns.

'How far are we from the trenches?' someone asked. Sergeant Molloy, who was pacing along their lines telling them to try and look like soldiers, heard. 'Far enough away so no nasty shells can reach us.' He paused and put his head on one side. 'Hear that?'

They could. From somewhere ahead, in the direction the train had been taking them, a rolling, rumbling thunder sounded. Guns.

William felt the hairs on the back of his neck prickle. Very soon, all his questions to himself would be answered.

Very soon, he'd find out if he could handle battle.

They marched to the camp. Yet another wait, and they were divided among the tents. They ate: a stew of tough, stringy meat. 'Horse,' grumbled someone, and William thought again of the sprawled, broken bodies.

Just as they were unrolling their blankets in the tents, fumbling in the gloom for packs to use as pillows, the eastern sky suddenly burst into flame. A second later, the noise came, like hundreds of metal doors slamming.

Jerry dived for the tent door, shouting. Herbert and Jack fell over each other as they followed. William hurdled them and stumbled into the open.

Men were pouring out of all the tents, staring in the same direction. The evening sky was on fire, shafts of white flickering and glaring, red and green stars bursting into light high up, then floating downwards, fading as they dropped. The noise drummed on. Then as suddenly as it had started, it stopped. A last gun fired; a final green flare drifted down. Darkness and silence filled the east again, except for a faraway rumble.

'Someone making a night attack?' Jack wondered.

'Maybe a sentry saw an enemy patrol,' another voice suggested.

Herbert shook his head. 'Whatever it was, I wouldn't want to be up there right now.'

Two nights later, they were.

Mr Gowing gave them the orders on their second morning. Further along the lines of tents, William could see other platoon commanders also talking to their men. 'We're moving up to the front tonight, chaps. We'll be taking over a nice quiet section of line and we'll be there for six days. This is what you've been waiting for, so make sure you're on your toes.' The young lieutenant couldn't keep the quiver out of his voice.

Blankets, spare clothes, any letters and papers that might give information to the enemy were to be left behind. They were fed an early dinner of more tough stew and onions. Rifles were inspected. So were boots and uniforms, to make sure no loose metal made a noise as they moved.

They were issued with bullets: a hundred rounds per man, in clips that they crammed into pouches and pockets. They were laden down with other gear: extra belts of bullets for machine-guns; empty sandbags; shovels; stretchers. 'Two steps with this lot, and I'll sink into the ground,' Jerry complained. Jack grinned at him. 'First you're grouching about sitting around. Now you're grouching about moving!' As darkness grew, they marched from camp, towards the east where flickers of white and red already jumped and flared along the horizon.

For three hours, they marched along narrow dirt roads. 'No talking!' rapped the NCOs. So there was silence, except for the tramp of boots, the creak of rifle slings, the occasional whisper coming back along the ranks: 'dead horse on the road ahead' . . . 'shell-hole on the right'.

William's back ached under the weight of pack, rifle and shovel, plus the box of Mills Bombs he and Jack held between them. When they finally halted, and were ordered to the side of the road, everyone sank down with sighs and groans.

The sound of approaching boots grew. Out of the darkness, lines of soldiers appeared, marching raggedly, some limping. Heads were bowed, shoulders bent. They straggled past, saying nothing, close enough for William

126 to see the worn, haggard faces. Would his platoon look like that after six days in the trenches?

In the next hours, they passed from tiredness to exhaustion, and from order to confusion. The night was so dark that they could see only the man in front of them. Guides who knew the trenches were leading them now and were supposed to take them to their section of the line. But the stops, the way they headed off down one muddy track, then had to turn and come back again, made it more and more clear that the guides were in trouble.

Muddy tracks were all they had now. The roads had ended. They trudged across fields where shells had torn the ground apart on every side. Water glinted in many of them. More smashed carts. The sickly-sweet smell of something rotting, and they filed past another dead horse, belly swollen, legs stiff and ugly.

After – five? six? – hours they were so weary, they could hardly keep their heads up. Their boots were thick with mud; every step was an effort. Necks ached and shoulders were raw from pack straps and ammunition belts. The box of Mills Bombs slung between Jack and William thudded against their legs, tripped them and sent them stumbling into the men ahead, who swore and complained. When another halt was called, they flopped down in the mud.

'We're lost,' voices muttered. 'We'll be caught in the open.'

William didn't want to think about that. The guns had been mostly quiet for the past hour. Just a couple of times one roared somewhere, over to their left, splitting the darkness with a spear of red-white. But if they hadn't reached their trenches by dawn, and the enemy saw them . . .

They struggled through a clump of splintered trees, stumbling over fallen branches, bumping into stumps. William could hear Herbert gasping for breath. His own body was one endless ache.

Across another field. Back again. If I meet that guide, I'm going to kick him right into the German lines, William told himself. But mostly he just plodded on, one step in front of another.

Yet another stop. They were never going to find their trenches. Any minute now, they'd be told to start digging, try to make some holes they could hide in like beasts. The ground ahead was uneven. Low ridges seemed to criss-cross it. What were—?

Next minute, they were climbing down wooden steps and into a trench. 'This way,' voices whispered. 'Hurry! This way.' They turned left, turned right, moved on.

Duckboards clacked under their feet. Walls of timber and sandbags rose on either side of them, high above their heads. Men with rifles stood on ledges, peering through slits in the sandbags. Others lay huddled in cramped alcoves cut into the trench walls, staring at 3 Platoon and the others as they filed past. They'd made it. Finally, they were there.

They had arrived just in time. Almost immediately, the

other troops in the trench began shrugging on packs, picking up rifles, forming up in lines to leave. They were in a hurry, also. Nobody wanted to be in the open when daylight came. The other soldiers were Scottish, by the sound of their accents. They whispered to William's platoon as they filed past, heading back in the direction the New Zealanders had come. 'Guid luck, laddie. . . There's a nasty wee German machine-gun o'er yon. Dinna stick your head up.'

Inside ten minutes, the trench was theirs. Sentries were posted and took their posts on the ledges – firing steps, William heard them called – staring into the darkness. William and Herbert found an empty alcove and lay down. William was exhausted, but knew he wouldn't sleep. He was too strung-out. He blinked as a green flare sailed high into the air above them. He—

The next flare was dull white, yet bright enough to fill the whole sky. It hung there, didn't fade. And something was hitting his foot. The Germans! Had they—? William's eyes flew open. A grey-white daylight was around him; Jack was standing there, gently (fairly gently) kicking his boot. 'Rise and shine, Will. You're on sentry in five minutes.'

William struggled to his feet. His arms still ached from carrying the Mills Bombs. His shoulders were sore; his eyes thick. He was hungry. Jack held a tin mug out to him. 'Three spoons of sugar in it. That'll keep you going.'

The tea was lukewarm, but it helped. By the time William was standing on the ledge, peering through the tiny slit in the wall of sandbags, he was fully awake. He blinked at the sight in front of him.

A tangle of barbed wire – coils and loops of it fixed to thick wooden stakes – curled chest-high in front of the trench. Beyond that, bare ground stretched away for a hundred yards or more, cratered with shell-holes, strewn with smashed bits of timber, a heap of broken bricks, the stumps of trees. Further away still, William could just make out more barbed wire, plus concrete or steel shapes rising from the ground like big grey drums. His breath caught as he realised it was the German front line.

Nothing moved in front of him. No Man's Land was still. But over there, eyes were watching in his direction. Watching and ready to shoot. William swallowed and gripped his rifle more tightly.

He stayed on sentry duty for two hours. A breakfast of cold tinned meat and bread was handed up to him in his mess tin. He ate it while he kept watching through the slit. His time was almost over when something twitched and moved just ten yards in front. A grey shape scuttled at him.

A yell rose in William's throat. The Huns! He jerked his rifle up, pointed it at the advancing German. The man must have been hiding somehow. How could he have—?

Then William realised. A rat. A grey rat, nearly the size of a kitten. It stopped just five yards away, seemed to stare straight at him. He saw its bald pink tail and pointed teeth. It darted sideways, and began pulling and chewing at a shape half-buried in the mud. Suddenly, William made out the shape of a human hand. He jerked his rifle again and the rat slunk away, dragging something with it. William heard himself gagging with disgust.

When his two hours were over, he stepped down into the trench and gazed around. Everything was grey or brown: duckboards, wooden or earth walls, sandbags, the crumpled shapes of men sleeping or sitting. The sky was grey. The faces of 3 Platoon looked grey as well. Everyone was filthy, from the trench or from stumbling and falling on their trek to the line. Everyone looked exhausted.

They became more exhausted as their first day passed. If they weren't on sentry duty, they were working. They carried boxes of ammunition. They levered buried duckboards out of sucking mud on the floor of the trench and shovelled drier earth underneath them. They strained to lift a heavy machine-gun and its tripod onto a platform in the next length of trench. They dug a deep chamber out of the rear wall and reinforced it with timber.

When Jerry asked what the space was for, Sergeant Molloy grunted, 'Just wait 'til there's an attack, lad. Then you'll see.' Jerry stared at William, who stared back as they both understood. Bodies.

Lunch was more cold meat, straight from the tin. They ate it sitting on the muddy duckboards. Already their uniforms and boots were caked with dirt. Their hands were filthy. They couldn't wash. 'Save your water,' an NCO came along the trench telling them. 'Drinking only – and not too much.'

All the while, the guns fired. Their artillery, well behind them now, booming and echoing. Enemy guns from far ahead. The first few times, everyone threw themselves face-down on the duckboards, while the sentries pressed against the walls. But after the first hours, they kept wearily going about their work, although heads still jerked at each explosion.

A few times, the snarl and rattle of machine-gun fire sounded, somewhere off to their left. But No Man's Land stayed empty. Nothing moved behind the German wire.

They were filling sandbags with dirt, to build their trench parapet higher, when a distant droning swelled to a roar, sentries shouted, and as everyone scrambled for their rifles, an aeroplane swept over the trench, low enough for William to glimpse the thick black crosses on its wings. A Hun!

Next moment, there was a burst of firing somewhere behind them. Yells and screams rose. The aircraft noise faded for a moment, swelled again. Another rattle of shots. Jerry began hauling himself up the rear wall of the trench to see what was happening.

'Down!' Sergeant Molloy yelled. 'Get down!' Jerry had scarcely ducked his head when the air was shrill with the whine and crack of bullets, flashing past just above the parapet. Their platoon NCO strode over to the red-haired soldier, grabbed his tunic, shook him hard. 'You do that again, O'Brien, and I'll throw you over the parapet so the enemy can have an easier shot. What sort of a blithering idiot are you?'

The sergeant's words were lost as their artillery all opened up at once. William's hands flew to his ears as the sound slammed at them. All along the trench, men crouched, trying to cover their heads. Sergeant Molloy was shoving at them. 'Stand up! Ready to fire! Sentries, watch the front!'

Ten minutes later, as the guns still crashed, a group of men half-stumbled, half-fell into the trench from the open ground behind. William recognised the New Zealand shoulder badges. One held a hand to his face; blood streamed between his fingers. Two others dragged a third between them, his body flopping.

A First Aid party hurried up. Some led the wounded soldier away. Others knelt over the unmoving man. They spoke to him, felt at his neck, then shook their heads. A blanket appeared from somewhere and was spread over his face and chest where he sprawled on the filthy duckboards.

For the next half-hour, until a stretcher party came to carry the body away, William kept glancing at the legs in their puttees and boots, lolling limply from under the blanket. I've seen my first dead man, he thought. It looks ugly and . . . and useless.

A supply party had been caught in the open. The news came down the trench as time passed. The German aeroplane had seen an easy target and attacked. 'No three-course dinner for you lot tonight,' Sergeant Molloy told them as he passed. 'Eat your spare socks if you get hungry.'

134   The rest of their six days in the trenches were much like the first. Hours of dirt, hunger, discomfort and boredom. Then a few wild minutes of noise and fear. Then dirt and boredom again.

On the second afternoon, as William huddled in his muddy sleeping space, yawning and hungry, yells swept along the trench. 'Gas! Gas!' Next minute, men were hurling themselves at their packs, dragging out the clumsy gas-masks, jamming them over their faces. Nothing happened. A sentry had seen the smoke from a cooking fire, and panicked.

On the third night, orders came to double up the sentries. A password was issued: *Farm Gate*. As darkness grew, the trench was lined with men, eyes straining through the slits between sandbags. Something must be happening, but nobody knew what.

Those trying to sleep lay with a hand on their rifles. 'Just make sure it's not pointing at me, chum,' Jack told Jerry as they huddled against the trench wall. 'Tell it I'm on your side.' Jerry managed a tired grin.

Hours passed. William's turn for sentry duty came. He stood on the firing step, shifting from foot to foot, trying to see. Had a shadow moved? No. Was that a man? No, a wooden stake. 'Farm Gate,' he murmured to himself. 'Farm Gate.' If he did see a man, if he called out 'Farm' and the figure didn't answer 'Gate', could he make himself shoot?

The blackness exploded into light. German guns were firing. Flashes of flame, fountains of dirt burst out all across No Man's Land. The ground was lit as bright as day. William glimpsed rats scurrying into shell-holes. Then darkness again. More explosions, more glares of light. Machine-guns hammered, not far away. Rifles cracked.

William heard the sentries further along calling out: 'See anything?' 'Nothing!' Their own artillery burst out, in a madhouse of noise and white-red fire. William pressed himself against the trench wall and waited for the world to end.

It didn't. After ten minutes, the noise faded. Occasionally a rifle shot rang out. A few flares rose, glowed, faded. William's two hours ticked away. In the morning, they learned that a raiding party had set out from their lines to attack the enemy trenches. Nobody knew how many were dead or wounded. Muddle and mess and mix-ups, William told himself. That's what war mostly seems to be.

He didn't feel a hero in the trenches. He was too tired, dirty, hungry. Staying awake and ready took all his energy. One look at the yawning, filthy faces of the others showed they were the same.

On the fourth night, there were strange creaking noises somewhere behind the German lines. The sentries were more nervous than usual. Mr Gowing came along the trench, looking as exhausted as everyone else. 'Keep alert, chaps. Something could be up.'

Something *was* up. They saw when daylight came. A big observation balloon, floating high above the enemy trenches on the end of a wire cable. A big black basket hung below it.

'There'll be an observer in that,' someone muttered.

'He'll see exactly where we are. He can signal their guns where to fire.' The balloon was far out of rifle range. William stared up helplessly.

But not for long. The sound of another aeroplane grew, from their side this time. Circles of red, white and blue on its wings, it droned over their heads and flew in a slow circle around the balloon.

William caught his breath as a tiny shape dropped from the basket beneath the balloon, plummeting towards the ground. White fluttered above it, a parachute spread, and the shape became a man, drifting down behind the German trenches. He lifted a hand to the British aeroplane, which circled again, then flew straight at the balloon. Flashes flickered from the plane. The balloon crumpled and began tumbling to earth.

He didn't kill him, William realised as he watched. The pilot could have killed that man, yet he let him live. And the German observer knew it. I've seen something generous and noble, William thought. Or something pointless and foolish.

137

That afternoon, it began to rain. Gently at first, then a steady downpour. Men huddled under waterproof capes that turned out not to be waterproof. Rain dripped from the back of William's helmet down his neck, dribbled down his sleeves, seeped inside his boots. The bottom of the trench became porridge-like mud, then ankle-high water. Rain drove into the alcoves where men tried to shelter or sleep. It poured down the walls in streams. By evening, work parties with buckets were bailing water from the deepest parts, sloshing it out onto the ground behind. Half of it poured straight back in. The rain kept falling. 'I didn't join the Army to go swimming, either,' Jerry grunted.

They chewed on stale bread and stringy cold bacon for tea. William was soaked through. His feet squelched in his boots. Under his cape, his tunic and shirt were plastered to his back. He gazed at the dripping faces of the others and wondered if he would ever be so miserable in his life again.

The downpour continued through the night. On sentry duty, William couldn't see a thing, couldn't hear a thing. Any enemy who tried to attack tonight would probably drown in No Man's Land. Even the guns were fairly quiet: just a few bursts of roaring fire now and

then. William was so exhausted that when Jerry came to take his place, he crawled into the sodden, filthy alcove in the trench wall and fell straight asleep.

By morning, No Man's Land had become a chaos of shell-holes filled to the brim with clay-coloured water, and stretches of liquid mud in between. Not even the rats were around. Still the rain fell.

About two hours after breakfast (bread so wet, it fell apart in their hands, plus tea that was half rainwater), a squad of men floundered down the trench, shin-deep in the slush, dragging two heavy boxes. They spoke to Sergeant Molloy, then splashed off again.

The sergeant called to William, who was nearest. 'Help me open these, lad.'

Rain pouring off them, they levered open the boxes with the tip of William's bayonet. He stared at what lay inside. Wicked-looking long knives and wooden clubs whose heads were studded with metal knobs and spikes.

Sergeant Molloy's face was grim. 'Trench-raiding weapons. Must be our turn next.' He squinted up into the driving rain. 'Better hope the weather stays this bad.'

It didn't. It got even worse. By evening, half of 3 Platoon were trying to bail out their section of trench. The water was up to their knees. Gear had vanished under the dirty water. Men stumbled, became stuck in the mud, fell full-length into the filthy muck.

There was no food, no dry clothing. As darkness came, the rain thrashed down. William almost welcomed his two hours on sentry duty; at least most of him was above the water. For the rest of the night, he leaned against the trench wall, gripping his rifle so it didn't fall into the water, head down, sunk in misery. If the Germans attacked now . . . but perhaps the Germans were just as wretched.

Just before dawn, the rain stopped suddenly. The sun rose in a bright blue sky, with a few white clouds at the edges. But the trench and No Man's Land were still oozing swamps.

'Wonder if the generals have any idea what it's like up here,' Jerry muttered as he and Jack tried to squeeze water from their tunics.

Herbert shrugged. 'Some of them haven't ever been near the front. They just look at photos.'

They were relieved the next night – by Australian soldiers, already filthy and tired from the long march up. 'Never thought I'd be glad to see an Aussie,' Jack grinned. There was no moon, thank goodness, and this time their guides seemed to know the way. Heads down, bodies weary, they struggled back over the muddy fields, through the shattered trees, onto the narrow road. I've been in the trenches, William told himself as he trudged along. I've seen war. But he was too exhausted to care.

140

They reached the safety of the rear lines just after daybreak. As they marched the last couple of miles, they stared around them. Guns stood in every group of trees, hidden from the air. Piles of shells lay nearby. Every building with a roof was full of troops, resting or checking gear. Horses stood in lines behind every wall.

A long line of ambulances drove past, down into a gulley where they couldn't easily be seen.

'What's going on?' William wondered.

It was Herbert who answered him. 'There's an attack being planned. A big one.'

Dearest Ma,

I know you'll never get this letter.

I'm writing it inside my head, the way Archie showed me. I asked for paper and pen so I could tell you I'm alive and unhurt, but prisoners here aren't allowed to write letters.

I'm in France, in a camp near the rear lines. They say I'll soon be taken up to the trenches – the battlefield – among the troops. Sometimes I've been told that I'll be stood out in the open where the enemy can see and shoot me, I think the Army hope they can frighten me into carrying out their orders. Or they're trying to make me feel so ashamed that I'll give up and obey them.

I am frightened. I'd be lying if I said I wasn't. But it's not fear of being killed. It's fear that I may give in; I've lasted this far. I'm sure others who oppose war like me have put up with much more. I don't want to let them down now.

There are NZ soldiers nearby. The guards mentioned them, and I've seen them passing by the place where I'm held. I keep looking for William. I just want to wish him well.

There is talk of a great attack coming very soon, and I hope with all my heart that he comes through safely. Perhaps it's better that I can't send you this letter, dear Ma! It would only give you even more to worry about.

Dearest Ma, I think of you and little (still ha-ha!) Jessie so much. I hope that someday all four of us will be together again. Until that happens, I will hold you in my heart, to help me be strong.

Your Loving Son

Edmund

Edmund

He was taken to France by train and boat. The morning after Corporal McKean told him he would be going, boots tramped outside his cell before it was properly light. The door opened, and he was ordered into the corridor. A two-man escort led him to a bigger, brighter room where the Camp Commandant, Colonel Brabin, sat.

'Atten-*shun!*' The escort's boots crashed together. Edmund stood as he was. In the last couple of days, his cold had become a fever. He felt weak and shaky, but he made himself stand as straight as possible and nodded to the officer. 'Good morning.'

Colonel Brabin surveyed him coldly. 'Have you any complaints about the way you've been treated here, Hayes?'

The question sounded so silly that Edmund almost laughed. But he kept his face blank and just shook his head slightly. 'You've done your best.'

The colonel glared at him as though Edmund were being cheeky. 'You're being moved from this camp to where you'll have your last chance to act like a man.' He paused. Edmund kept watching him, but said nothing. After a few seconds, Colonel Brabin jerked his head. 'Take him away.'

For two hours or more, Edmund and his escort waited by the camp gate. Soldiers passing by looked at him curiously or joked with the soldiers guarding him. 'He looks fierce . . . You afraid he'll bite?'

He dozed on the train, his hot head bumping against the cool window glass. At a port noisy with wheels, whistles and men yelling orders, his escort marched him out onto a wharf, then stood looking around uncertainly.

Corporal McKean appeared. 'Put the handcuffs on him.' As the soldiers hesitated, and Edmund opened his mouth to protest, the NCO shouted: 'Obey the order! Put the cuffs on him!'

The steel bracelets were clamped on his wrists. He was marched along the wharf and up a gangway onto a ship. He tried to keep his head up as he'd done before, but tiredness and loneliness dragged at him. What chance did he have against the great machine of the Army? Without Archie, or anyone else who felt the same way, he was helpless and feeble. Perhaps it was time to give up after all.

Edmund was locked in a tiny storeroom and saw nothing of the short voyage across the English Channel. He felt the floor shudder under his feet as the engines turned, the slowing down and the slight jolt as they docked. For an hour after that, feet tramped overhead: the soldiers being moved off. Then his escort appeared, took him down to the wharf and along to a truck piled high with boxes of vegetables.

'We'll take the cuffs off you, chum,' one soldier said. 'But if the corp turns up, they'll have to go back on.'

Edmund stood by the truck, rubbing his wrists where the metal had pinched them. After a while, they all climbed up and sat among the crates. When the truck moved off in a long line of vehicles an hour later, there was still no sign of the NCO.

They drove all through the afternoon. It was almost like taking the market garden vegetables to the shops. Edmund wondered how Mr Yee was and if he would ever work there again. He felt himself growing sleepy. His body still shook sometimes with fever.

At first the road was straight and level, with lines of poplar trees on each side. But then great holes began to appear in the fields around them, craters with soil flung in all directions. The trucks slowed and jolted as

they edged around other holes in the road. Men in grey uniforms, with shovels and wooden barrows, were filling some, while a couple of soldiers in dark blue leaned on their rifles, watching. Germans and their French guards, Edmund realised. He and his escort stared as the convoy crawled on.

Progress got even slower. Most of the farmhouses

they passed now were damaged or ruined, roofs and walls smashed. In the deep ditches beside the roads, wrecked carts lay. A couple of times, there were dead mules or horses as well, bodies swollen, mouths open and tongues lolling. Black clouds of flies circled them. The smell was like rotting apples.

Further on, the fields were just swamps. Drains and streams had been blocked by bursting shells, or their banks had been destroyed so they poured onto the land. An old man and woman stood at the edge of one flooded field where two dead cows half-floated. The old woman was crying.

It was evening when they ground through a gate in a high wire fence, past sentries in British uniforms. Tents, a few bare buildings, paths of muddy duckboards, more open areas with troops marching across them. Yet another army camp.

But this one was different in two ways. Now that the truck had stopped, Edmund could hear the deep rumbling and growling from somewhere up ahead. He knew what the sound was: the artillery of the battlefield.

The other difference was on one of the areas where men were marching. A wooden post, higher than a man, set into the ground. Edmund knew what that was as well.

Corporal McKean was waiting for them. 'Why isn't the prisoner handcuffed?' he snapped at the escort.

As they started to reply, he jabbed a finger at Edmund. 'You have no rights here, conchie. None at all. Nobody's going to worry if something happens to you. Nobody's going to miss you. There's no-one for you to run to.'

Edmund said nothing. He held out his wrists for the handcuffs. He and the escort stood there while other soldiers unloaded the crates and carried them to a nearby building with smoke rising from a tin chimney. He gazed around, hoping to see some sign of the other COs. But there was none. His heart began to sink again. His head ached; his body kept shivering.

He was taken to yet another bare office, yet another table with yet another officer – a sandy-haired major with glasses. The man ignored Edmund at first; kept scribbling on a sheet of paper. Then he looked up. 'What's this one's name?'

148

The escort snapped to attention, and one of them opened his mouth. But Edmund spoke first. Archie's words came to him again, and he made sure he stayed polite. 'Good evening. I'm Edmund Hayes.'

The major looked annoyed. 'There's nothing special about you, you realise, Hayes.'

Edmund nodded. 'I know. I'm just one of many who feel the same way.'

A glare. 'There are New Zealanders fighting near here. Your countrymen. They're crack troops. Don't you feel ashamed that you're a coward and you're letting them down?'

New Zealanders. One face was instantly in Edmund's mind. Could he ask – no, of course not. He realised the major was still glaring at him. 'No, I'm not ashamed. I want this war to stop so their friends and families can see them come home safely.'

'Don't try and be clever with me, Hayes!' Oh, why do people think I'm being clever? Edmund sighed. I'm only trying to answer the questions. His head ached; he tried to concentrate on what the sandy-haired officer was saying to him.

'We're not going to shoot you, Hayes. That's the easy way out. We're not going to make a martyr out of you.'

Edmund couldn't decide what to say. He felt too tired to be grateful, but he heard himself say 'Thank you.'

The major must have thought he was being clever again. 'We're going to break you instead. You're in army uniform. You're in an army camp. You'll be given orders like any soldier. The penalties for refusing to obey those orders are severe, I'll tell you that right now. They include death by firing squad.'

In spite of his sick tiredness, Edmund half-smiled.

'You mean you won't shoot me, but you'll have me shot?'

The major banged a fist down on the table. 'Move, you men!' he shouted at Edmund's escort. 'Put him in the cells!'

It wasn't a proper cell. Just a room on the end of a bigger building, with a padlock on the door. Darkness grew. No food. Edmund was so tired that he didn't want to eat anyway. He still felt lonely and helpless. In spite of what he'd said to the major, he didn't know how much longer he could last by himself.

He sat with his back against a wall and dozed. In the distance, the guns rumbled on. Sometime later, he jolted awake to boots tramping past outside. Soldiers, hundreds of them by the sound of it.

In the morning, he felt a little better. A mess tin of watery stew was brought to him and a mug of dark-brown tea. He swallowed them both eagerly.

A two-man escort, different soldiers from yesterday (the Army must be afraid I'll pass on conscientious objector germs if I'm with any of them too long, he decided) took him outside. All around the camp, troops were bustling and moving. His guards had just taken up position on either side of him when a line of soldiers came around the corner.

These ones weren't marching. They were shambling, stumbling. Their faces were haggard; their uniforms filthy with mud. They reeled as they moved. Some trudged along with eyes closed. They held their rifles crookedly; some weapons were almost dragging on the ground.

'Just back from the trenches,' murmured one of Edmund's escort, while they stared.

As they came past, one man staggered. His knees buckled and he lurched sideways. He was going to fall.

Without thinking, Edmund stepped forward and seized him. He put one arm around the soldier's shoulders, grabbed the rifle with his other as it fell from the soldier's grasp. The soldier sagged against him, while Edmund struggled to hold him upright.

Then the escort and two of the man's companions gripped him and steadied him until he was standing shakily upright. His eyes flickered open. He stared around in confusion and embarrassment. 'Sorry. I . . . sorry.'

The other two mud-caked soldiers slung their exhausted comrade's arms over their shoulders. 'Thanks, chum,' one mumbled to Edmund. 'OK, Dick. Just another few yards,' he told the slumped figure between them as they began to move on.

For a moment, Edmund stood there. He seemed to see himself from the outside. Someone dressed in an army uniform. Someone holding a rifle. He stared at the weapon in his hand: the long steel barrel, the smooth wooden butt, the snug bolt and chunky magazine of bullets. Quickly he thrust it at one of the escort. 'Here!'

The soldier jerked backwards. Then he took the rifle and slung it over his shoulder. He grinned at Edmund. 'Thanks for not shooting us, pal.'

Edmund didn't know what to think.

They marched him on. Another show-and-be-ashamed around another camp, Edmund supposed.

No. They turned a corner, turned a second, and came to the building with the tin chimney, the one into which the boxes of vegetables had been carried yesterday. One of the guards took a quick look around and nodded to the other. They opened the door, and Edmund was inside the cookhouse.

Cooks were cutting up chunks of meat, peeling potatoes, stoking the fires of three huge stoves. They glanced up as escort and prisoner came in, then carried on with their work.

'Cup of tea time,' one guard announced. He headed for the stoves, where big dixies bubbled. The other leaned his rifle and the one Edmund had handed him against a table, and sat where he could see through the window.

'Sit yourself down, pal. If any officers are coming, we'll march you out of here fast enough.'

Edmund sat gratefully. He still felt weak, although his cold and fever seemed less. The first soldier returned, with two steaming mugs. He handed one to Edmund. 'Get that down you, pal.' Tears filled Edmund's eyes suddenly. It was kindness, not harshness, that almost undid him.

For ten minutes, they just sat and talked. Edmund remembered the camp in England and the other soldiers behind the barn. These ones also wanted to know why he'd chosen to stand against the war. He told them, as briefly as he could, and they nodded. 'Makes sense,' one said. 'But nobody's going to listen to you.'

'I still—' Edmund began. Then a cook, a middle-aged man, called to them. 'Give us a hand with these dixies, lads.' The guards rose, moved across, and helped heave some of the big pots off the stove. Edmund hesitated, then stayed where he was.

The cook saw him. 'What's the matter with you?'

'I'm sorry,' Edmund said. 'I can't obey any army order. I don't mean to be rude.'

The cook's face changed. 'You drink my tea, but you won't even help with this? Get out! Now!'

The escort picked up their rifles and led Edmund outside. Their expressions weren't so friendly any more. 'Can't you just help a bloke who needs it?' one demanded.

And 'His son was killed last year. On a ship that got sunk,' grunted the other.

I did help someone who needed it, Edmund thought. Just quarter of an hour ago. But he stayed silent. There were more and more times when things didn't seem clear, when he didn't know if he'd behaved the right way. He felt tired and worn-out again.

Back in the storeroom cell an hour later, Edmund thought of the soldiers and officers he had met in the past months. Those who had shouted at him or tripped him. Those who had given him fruit and chocolate. The Army has good people, he told himself. I know that now. Good people with good reasons for being here, even if I can't ever agree. After all, William is one of them.

There was a blanket in his cell now. He wrapped it around himself and sat against the wall. In the distance, the guns muttered. He felt shaky and unwell again, but he tried to recite some of the poems he and Archie had taught each other. What had happened to the other COs? Had they given in?

154

The door swung open. Corporal McKean glowered at him. 'On your feet. Time to see what you're made of.'

Yesterday's sandy-haired major sat behind the same table. 'You're being given one last chance, Hayes.

I strongly suggest you take it.' He paused. Edmund said nothing.

'There is ammunition that needs cleaning before it's taken up to the front. You will clean it.'

Another pause. Edmund shook his head. 'I can't accept that order.'

The major watched him coldly for a few seconds, then spoke to Corporal McKean. 'This man is sentenced to three hours of Field Punishment No. 1, followed by solitary confinement. See to it.'

'Sir!' The corporal seized Edmund's elbow and pushed him out of the room. Edmund knew what was coming.

Corporal McKean and three soldiers marched him across the flat area where troops had been drilling the day before. The tall wooden post stood ahead.

They halted in front of it. 'Turn around,' snapped the NCO. 'Hands behind you.'

155

For a moment, Edmund thought of refusing. But it would do no good. He turned so his back was against the post and held his arms out behind him.

'Tie them together,' the corporal ordered. Edmund felt something around his wrists. 'Tighter!' The rope cut into his flesh.

'Now tie his hands and ankles to the post,' Corporal McKean rapped.

A soldier muttered, 'Move back, chum', and Edmund took half a step backwards until his heels were touching the base of the post. Another rope was passed around his ankles and drawn tight. His bound hands were drawn back, too.

'Higher!' went Corporal McKean. As one of the soldiers began to say something, the NCO shouted, 'I said higher! That's an order!' Edmund's hands were pulled up behind him until they were nearly as high as his neck. The pain in his shoulders made him gasp.

The corporal stood in front of him. The rest of the men stared at the ground. 'You were warned, Hayes. We'll be back in three hours. Enjoy yourself.' He barked a command at the escort, and all four marched away.

His feet weren't so bad, Edmund realised. The rope hurt his ankles, but he could shuffle an inch or two. But his arms, twisted up behind him, were already agony. They felt as though they were about to burst out of their shoulder sockets. He tried to move them, slide them down the post. He almost cried out loud as pain surged through him.

After five minutes, he knew he couldn't stand it. If he lifted his heels from the ground, the drag on his arms was slightly less. But then his whole body began to cramp and spasm. Every muscle from knee to neck seemed to be wrenching apart. He lowered his heels to the ground once more, and instantly the pain in his arms and shoulders clawed at him.

He couldn't feel his hands any longer. The ropes must be cutting off circulation in his wrists. But the muscles of his arms burned with agony. I have to call for help. I have to give in and do whatever the Army orders. He opened his mouth to shout.

He stopped. That soldier yesterday. He'd endured hours or days of suffering, Edmund thought, and I'm going to give up after just a few minutes? And my letters to Ma. I told her I was going to keep going. Now the test is here; I have to face it.

His eyes were closed, his teeth clenched. The bones of his elbows and wrists felt as though they might snap at any moment. Fangs seemed to be ripping at his shoulders. Once in a play fight when they were children, William had twisted Edmund's arms up behind his back, and Edmund had screamed with the pain. This was ten times worse. Even though he tried not to move, hands seemed to grip his body, torturing every part of it.

157

He began to count. 'One . . . two . . .' Up to ten, standing on his toes so the pain beat through his back. 'Eleven . . . twelve . . .' Another ten with heels down, while his arms tore and throbbed. His neck was hurting too now. So were the muscles of his legs, cramping and burning as he tried to find some relief from the agony.

There were voices nearby. Corporal McKean was back: the 'three hours' was just to scare him and make him give in. No. When he opened his eyes, some troops were crossing the flat ground about twenty yards away, staring at him, muttering among themselves. Edmund tried to lift his head and look back at them, but the pain was too much.

Somehow time passed. After . . . he didn't know how long . . . his back seemed to have lost nearly all feeling. His arms still hurt so dreadfully that his jaws ached from clenching his teeth together. Will I ever be able to move properly again? he wondered.

His head hung forward. He didn't have any strength left to try and hold himself upright. Another voice was shouting orders. Edmund forced his eyes open and saw a group of German prisoners being marched past. They stared, too, fear in their faces. Did they think that this would happen to them? A sudden flash of agony shot through him as he tried to move. A voice cried 'Ahhh!' His voice.

He must have fainted. The next thing he knew, he was hanging forward on the ropes, his entire body throbbing. His arms felt dead. His feet didn't seem to belong to him.

Corporal McKean was there, with the escort. It was really him this time. The NCO jerked his head at the other soldiers. 'Cut him down.'

The moment the ropes around his ankles and wrists were gone, Edmund collapsed on the ground. One soldier tried to grab him, but he landed face-down, felt the earth in his nostrils and mouth. He couldn't move, just lay there with arms still stretched out crookedly behind him. The pain was worse than ever.

'Get up!' The corporal's voice. Edmund tried to stir, but couldn't. His arms were dead. 'Get up!' Then – 'All right, you can crawl back to your cell.'

Another voice spoke. 'Look at the poor sod, Corp. He can't do anything.' Then hands were helping him to his feet. Edmund almost screamed as his arms were lifted over others' shoulders, and they began to half-carry him across the ground. He glimpsed the face of Corporal McKean, tight and angry, but the NCO did nothing to stop the others.

They got him into his cell and lowered him to the ground. Someone spread the blanket over him. 'Poor sod,' a voice said again. The door closed. Alone on the bare floor, Edmund began to weep.

He couldn't sleep that night. Just lying there was agony. Trying to move was unbearable. Sometime he became aware that a mess tin of bread and cheese was beside him. He tried to take a piece, but groaned as the pain shot through him.

Outside, something was happening. All through the hours of darkness, he heard the tramp of feet as men marched past. Heavy wheels rumbled. Horses neighed. The whole camp seemed to be moving. But he was in too much pain to care. He lay curled on the cold floor, trying to think of home, and his mother and sister. And of his brother. If William could see him now, what would he say?

It was raining in the morning. Edmund heard it drumming on the roof of the cell, splashing on the ground outside. He'd finally managed to sit up, lean his back against the wall and drink the now-cold tea that had been standing there. His hands and arms shook so much he could hardly hold the mug. His body felt as though hammers had been pounding at it.

He half-lifted his head as Corporal McKean strode into the cell. He waited for the insults and sneers. But the NCO just looked at him. 'Can you walk?'

Edmund tried to stand, but sagged back. The corporal called over his shoulder. 'Bring him to the officer.'

Two different soldiers supported him to the major's office. His legs could move by themselves, but he reeled if he tried to stand. The major's face was still cold. 'I'm repeating yesterday's order, Hayes. Clean the amm—'

'No.' Edmund could hardly believe it was his voice. 'No.'

The major showed no expression. 'Three hours' Field Punishment No. 1. Take him away.'

The rain poured down as the escort took him to the post. Edmund could stumble along unaided by himself now – just. By the time they halted, he was already soaked through.

Corporal McKean spoke. 'You've made your point, Hayes. Obey the order, will you?'

The wish to give in was so great that Edmund had to close his eyes. But his voice seemed to speak by itself again: 'No.'

Again, the corporal looked at him. Then he spoke to the others. 'Tie him up.'

Today's soldiers said nothing. His legs were bound to the post. His arms were hauled up behind him, and he couldn't prevent a cry of pain. The NCO and escort moved off.

The pain was different from the first time, deeper and heavier somehow. His body seemed to be dragged at by racks and wheels, wrenching it in all directions. He didn't try to change his position any longer. Nothing would stop the agony.

His head flopped forward. Rain drove down on him, poured off his face, streamed down his back. His fever had returned: he felt hot and sick in spite of the rain. Darkness rose in his mind. The world began to fade. Pain still throbbed through him, but it seemed further and further away with each second. Even the rain seemed to fall without touching him. Suddenly, Edmund heard a voice speak quietly inside his head. His own voice. 'I'm going to die.'

Then hands were holding him, and other, angry voices were shouting. The ropes no longer bound him. He began to fall forward again, but this time he was seized and kept half-standing. 'It's not right!' a Scottish accent was saying. A different voice shouted: 'You don't treat a *dog* like this!'

There were soldiers all around him. Wet and dirty, rifles over their shoulders. They looked like the ones of two days ago, back from the front lines. 'What's going on?' they demanded. 'What the hell are you doing to him?'

Corporal McKean appeared, pushing his way through. 'This man is undergoing No. 1 Field Punishment. Stand back!'

But the soldiers who had cut Edmund down were

having none of it. 'Look at the poor devil! You trying to kill him? It's not right!'

The corporal glared around. He turned to the escort, standing nervously behind him. 'Take the prisoner back to his cell.'

They had to carry Edmund this time. He had no strength left at all. The other soldiers followed. 'This what we're fighting for, is it? . . . Tie *you* up! See how you like it!'

He'd been lying on the floor of his cell for maybe ten minutes, wet, wretched, racked with pain, when Corporal McKean came in once more. He carried two more blankets, which he dropped on the ground beside Edmund. Then the NCO stood looking down at his prisoner. There was an expression on his face that Edmund hadn't seen before.

'I don't know what to make of you, Hayes,' the corporal said. 'I really don't.'

He began to leave, then paused. 'There'll be some food in a few minutes. Eat it if you can. Try to sleep. There's something big going to happen up at the front, and you're coming up there with us tomorrow.'

163

PART 6

FIRST ATTACK

Dearest Ma,

Another letter inside my head. Another letter I'm glad you'll never get.

Dear Ma, I've seen terrible things. I've seen the bodies of dead men, and other men who wished they were dead. I've seen land that looks as though a monster has torn it apart.

This is a world where humans live like beasts, and where the killing goes on day and night. I never knew some men could do such dreadful things to one another, and I never knew some men could be so kind and brave.

I've done things I never believed I would do. If I ever see you again, I wonder if I'll be able to tell you about them. I pray you and Jessie are well. I pray William is safe. I believe I will die here, but I hope that you three will someday be together and happy once more.

Your Loving Son

Edmund

Edmund

He was marched up to the front lines the following night. In the growing darkness, he and Corporal McKean and two soldiers with rifles and bayonets made their way along a rough, shell-holed road and across what seemed to be fields.

Several times as they trudged on, the cool night was filled with a sickly-sweet smell and they glimpsed dead horses lying among smashed carts. A few shattered walls showed where farmhouses had once stood. Beside one wall were five small oblong mounds of earth in a neat row. Graves, Edmund realised.

Several times the corporal stopped other soldiers to ask for directions. Then they backtracked, or struck off in a different direction, or went a few yards and stood peering around them in the darkness.

If he'd wanted to, Edmund could probably have slipped off and vanished from the escort's sight. But where will I go to? he asked himself. Anyway, I'm not going to run away – I'm not going to let Archie and the others down like that.

After the first hour, he was too exhausted to run anywhere. Too exhausted to walk, almost. His body still ached from the hours tied to the post. His neck and arms and back felt as though horses had been pulling him apart.

As the ground became muddier, and they slipped and stumbled into holes, or on greasy duckboards, he could hardly put one foot in front of another. His head was bowed. He plodded on, scarcely noticing where they were, the torn-up ground blurring in front of him. His fever seemed to have returned; he felt sick and giddy. Three times the escort had to stop and wait for him while he hunched over, shaking and gasping. Corporal McKean watched, but said nothing.

Their feet clattered across more duckboards, covered with rough wire-netting this time. Nails stuck up here and there; Edmund caught his foot on one and stumbled.

Sometime around midnight, they slumped down on a low bank in the darkness to rest and eat. A few stunted bushes clung to the torn ground nearby. Off to one side, guns thumped and boomed. Flashes of flame split the night for a second. But around them, all was silent.

Edmund sprawled sideways on the wet earth. He had no food; felt too tired to care. The corporal began to chew on a piece of bread, hesitated, then tore off half and handed it to Edmund. 'You're a fool, Hayes. If everyone behaved like you, how could we have an army?'

Edmund nodded, his neck stabbing as he did so. 'You couldn't. That's the point.'

The NCO glared at him, then turned to the escort. 'Come on – on your feet. Get moving!' As they stood, he pushed another chunk of bread at Edmund. 'Here – eat this.'

They plodded on. Another hour – two hours? Edmund was too confused and shaky to tell – and they made their way down rough steps into a deep trench. Another corporal was waiting for them. Edmund wondered how many officers and NCOs he'd faced since that Monday morning in Mr Yee's garden. 'The prisoner?' asked this one. 'Bring him along here.'

They zigzagged their way up the network of trenches. Men were all around them now, standing on ledges, peering through holes in the sandbags stacked along the parapets, sleeping or sitting in recesses dug from the trench walls, squeezing past in the opposite direction, carrying boxes and stretchers. Other troops with ladders or coils of barbed wire inched by. Edmund remembered Corporal McKean's words from the day before. Something big was about to happen, all right.

A few men stared at Edmund and his escort, but most seemed too busy or tired to take any notice. The sickly-sweet smell of dead horses hung around the trench, but Edmund knew without being told that it wasn't horses this time. He thought yet again of William. What had happened to him? Was he . . . was he still alive? He *had* to be.

The new NCO led them through a tunnel, beneath a roof of thick wooden beams covered with earth, and into a big dug-out where dixies steamed on steel bars, over a fire of broken timber. 'Wait there. I'll fetch the CSM.'

Corporal McKean and the others dug into their packs, brought out mess tins, and dipped them into a dixie from which the smell of stew drifted. 'Tea in the other,' called out a soldier who was peeling carrots on a grubby table. He looked curiously at Edmund. 'Help yourself, chum.'

'Go on, Hayes,' Corporal McKean said as his prisoner hesitated. 'Get a mug from over there.'

Edmund hesitated another moment. Did this mean he was obeying an army order? And did he have any right to eat food meant for men who had come here prepared to die?

Before he could decide, the other corporal was back. Behind him came a burly man with bristling black hair. Corporal McKean and the escort quickly stood, still holding their mess tins.

'This the conchie?' growled the newcomer.

'Yes, sergeant-major,' replied the corporal. 'He's—'

'He's nothing,' the CSM interrupted. 'He's rubbish.' He thrust his face forward until it was almost touching Edmund's. 'We've got another conchie up here. He tried to get clever with us – wouldn't march when he was ordered. So he was dragged across the duckboards to wake his ideas up a bit. He just lay there like a coward and took it. You a coward, too, conchie?'

Edmund's temper rose. 'Being a conscientious objector doesn't make you a coward. It—'

A thick fist smashed against the side of his face. He staggered sideways. White lights seemed to explode in front of his eyes; there was a ringing inside his skull. He clutched at the trench wall. Then a boot kicked his legs from under him, and he collapsed onto the duckboards. His head throbbed; his sore back sent a shaft of pain through him.

The escort and the cooks stood staring. Corporal McKean stepped forward. 'The prisoner has given no trouble, CSM. He's been co-operative.'

The sergeant-major sneered. 'You on his side, are you, Corporal? Conchies are cowards, and that's the way I treat cowards.'

Painfully, Edmund struggled to his feet. He steadied himself with one hand against the side of the trench, and looked straight at the CSM. 'Why did you do that? I've never done you any harm. Why do you treat another man like that?'

The other man's face flushed. He pulled his arm back for another punch. Edmund whipped a hand forward, seized the thick wrist and held it. All the strength of the market garden and prison quarry days seemed to come flooding back into his aching body. He pushed the CSM's fist aside.

'I don't believe in war!' He felt startled at the anger in his voice. 'I won't obey orders to harm other men. But that doesn't mean I'll let you treat me like a dog. Stop it! Stop it now!'

The sergeant-major tore his fist out of Edmund's grasp. 'Take him to the ammunition dump. If he tries to escape, shoot him!' He spun around and stamped off up the trench.

Corporal McKean shook his head. 'You don't make things easy for yourself, do you, Hayes?' He glanced along the trench where the CSM had gone, then gazed at Edmund for a second. 'He's in charge of you now. Just think before you act, eh?'

Edmund's heart was still pounding from the rage he'd felt. He tried to speak calmly. 'Thank you, Corporal. Good luck to you.'

Corporal McKean watched him for another second. Then he turned, signalled to the escort and was gone.

Edmund began trudging along the trench, the other corporal close behind. His head still throbbed from the punch. The side of his face hurt when he touched it. His whole body ached. The strength that had flooded through it when he seized the CSM's wrist had vanished just as suddenly. He felt sick and shaky again.

The sergeant-major was waiting around the next corner of the trench. 'Don't think you're anyone special, conchie. We broke the other one and we'll break you. You're in uniform, so you're a soldier, understand?'

Edmund said nothing, which seemed to make the burly man angrier. 'If you get killed here, people will just think you'd joined up like any real man would. It's more than you deserve, rubbish like you.'

Edmund kept silent. 'Handcuff him!' the CSM ordered the corporal. 'He stays here. If he tries anything, you know what to do – though he's not even worth a bullet.'

The last hours of the night crawled past. Edmund lay huddled in a corner of the dug-out, his hands handcuffed to a heavy wooden box. 'Sorry, chum,' muttered the soldier who clamped the steel around his wrists. 'Orders is orders.'

More men pressed past, shoulders bent under the weight of weapons, belts of bullets, boxes. NCOs and officers urged them on in anxious whispers. 'Hurry! There's no time to spare!' The guns were largely silent; the world seemed to be waiting.

The sky was still half-dark when the CSM appeared, along with two armed soldiers. 'Bring him to the bomb dump' was all he said. The handcuffs were unlocked, and Edmund was led along another length of trench to a side passage. Heavy beams covered it. In the far corner, earth steps led up to the open air. Boxes were stacked on the floor. Troops were lifting objects from them: objects with wooden handles and metal heads shaped like pineapples.

The sergeant-major grinned. It was a grin that looked like a snarl. 'Mills Bombs,' he said. 'They make a nasty mess when they explode. I wouldn't want to be in here if a shell hits.'

He turned to the soldiers guarding Edmund. 'Pull a box over to the steps. Cuff him to it.'

Edmund opened his mouth, shut it again. The two guards glanced at each other. Then they dragged one of the heavy boxes across the dirt until it lay by the steps. Without looking at him, they fixed Edmund's handcuffs to the metal handles.

The sergeant-major grinned again. 'I'll see you later, conchie – if you're still in one piece.'

Then Edmund was alone, the deadly explosives all around him, a square of pink-and-blue dawn sky above. He sat down beside the box. So this is how things will end, he told himself. Blown to bits by a stray shell. No chance for Ma and Jessie to know the truth of what happened. I've come all this way, endured all this, for nothing.

He gazed up at the sky. It was pale with dawn light now. All around there was silence. A flicker high above made him glance up again. A flock of birds, black specks against the growing light, sped across the sky. No, they were— Then the world exploded.

All at the same moment, artillery slammed and bellowed. Hundreds of guns, thousands of them by the sound of it, blasting and roaring. The din was like great sheets of steel crashing together.

Then another explosion, so huge that Edmund was flung from where he sat onto the ground. The walls of the trench shook and earth cascaded down. The sky was blotted out as fountains of dirt and black smoke poured across it. Edmund clawed his way off the ground. Dear God, what had happened?

The artillery still boomed and bellowed. And now there were other noises. Whistles – lots of them, shrilling along the trenches on either side. Voices yelling. The crack of rifles. A wicked burst of shooting: *blat–blat–blat!* That must be a machine-gun. More whistles. Screams as well as yells. All the while, the thunder of the guns kept on. Deafened and shocked, Edmund crouched beside the box of bombs and tried to understand.

An attack. It must be. From the Germans or from the British, the New Zealanders? He had no idea. He remembered Corporal McKean's words: 'Something big's going to happen.' But this wasn't big. This was monstrous. This was inhuman.

Without warning, a calm spread through him. In the middle of all the noise, while explosions still boomed, shells tore overhead, and men yelled and howled in the distance, Edmund was completely still. A feeling of great love for his mother and sister flooded him. And for his brother. Right now, perhaps, William was fighting and dying out there. If we ever meet again, Edmund decided, we won't argue any more. Life is too precious for that.

The noise of the battle was changing. The shells landed further away. The machine-gun fire was less; the yells and rifle shots seemed more distant. It must be a British attack. Soldiers had left their trenches and were charging towards the German lines.

A whine, a *crack!* A shower of dirt and column of dark smoke made him duck his head. The enemy artillery were firing as well. I'm totally helpless here. If a shell lands in the trench, or even near . . . He stared down at the handcuffs and the box's metal handles. No way could he break free.

Another whine, another *crack!* But no black smoke this time. Instead, a dirty yellow cloud began creeping across the top of the trench. Edmund gaped. What was – then a puff of yellow drifted down to him. Instantly, his eyes stung and streamed. He gasped for breath. Gas!

His calm vanished. He was going to die like some

trapped animal. He wrenched at the box's handles, beat the handcuffs against its edge. 'Help!' he shouted. 'Hel—'

Another drift of gas, and the words choked in his throat.

Through streaming eyes, he saw a figure come rushing into the bomb dump. A figure with two huge blank eyes and a snout instead of a face. Someone in a gas mask. Then hands were shoving another mask over his head, pushing it tight against his nose and cheeks. Edmund gasped and coughed, bent over to drag in more air. He could breathe. The other man had vanished.

Time crawled past. Edmund sprawled beside the steps, wheezing and shocked. Black specks still arced across the sky, but the bombardment seemed to be further and further away. Rifles and machine-guns cracked, but they were more distant still. The blue sky was clouding over.

Two soldiers appeared. Edmund recognised the ones who had cuffed him to the box. 'Sit up, pal,' one panted. 'Time you were out of here.'

They unlocked the handcuffs. Edmund forced his aching body to sit. With shaking hands, he pulled off the hot, clammy gas mask. 'Did you – bring me that?'

The men looked surprised. 'Not us, chum. Too busy keeping our heads down.'

Edmund didn't know what to think.

There was no sign of the CSM. The two soldiers led him back through trenches that Corporal McKean had brought him along last night. Groups of men were filing down them, filthy, drained-looking, eyes staring. Some were held up by others. Some clutched arms from which blood dripped, or pressed hands to their faces as they staggered along. They've been in the attack, Edmund realised.

He stood against the trench wall as men carrying a stretcher struggled by. A limp shape lay on it, one arm trailing along the ground. Another stretcher followed: another still figure, with a tunic over its face.

One of the stretcher-bearers slipped, fought to keep his grip on the handles. Without thinking, Edmund grabbed one to steady the load. His sore arms throbbed with pain. 'Thanks, chum,' panted the bearer. Next minute, he and Edmund were carrying the silent load on down the trench.

The escort was left behind. Edmund glanced back, but couldn't see them. Will they think I'm trying to escape? he wondered. Will they shoot – no, they can't; not in here. Then the other stretcher-bearer gasped, 'This way', and Edmund looked around just as they began straining to lift their load up some clay steps.

At the top, other sprawled shapes lay beside a low bank where a few more half-smashed shrubs grew.

Edmund stood, gazing at the row of dead young men. How could people do this to one another?

'Hey?' A voice was calling to him. 'Hey, pal? Lend us a hand.' Edmund jerked. A soldier with a Red Cross armband was kneeling beside one of the bodies, covering it with a blanket. 'Let's make these poor devils decent. Might be days before we can take them back for burial.' He stared at Edmund, who was still looking at the row of motionless figures. 'All right?'

'All right,' said Edmund, and knelt to help.

They worked together, not speaking much, laying the grey blankets over man after man, tucking them under. A few spots of rain fell. More stretchers arrived; more bodies were laid on the ground. Sometimes the stretcher-bearers stood and watched for a few minutes. Sometimes they just turned and trudged away.

The rain began to fall harder. The guns were thumping again in the distance. Fresh bursts of rifle and machine-gun fire broke out, somewhere over to one side. After an hour or so, fewer stretcher-loads arrived.

The soldier with the Red Cross armband, a tall, thin man with a quiet voice, said, 'Check their tags will you, chum? I'll write them down.' When Edmund looked uncertain, the other man pointed. 'Their identity tags. Around their necks. We want a record of who the poor blokes are.'

Edmund's body still throbbed with pain, but slowly he began to move along the row of bodies, folding back blankets, opening shirts and tunics, trying not to look at ruined faces. He read aloud as the other man scribbled in a notebook, hunched over it to keep the rain off. 'Benton A. K., 758788, Third Manchester Regiment ... O'Neill P., 952286, Royal Irish Guards ... MacNeice L. R., 793518, Highland Light Infantry ...'

Then a voice sneered: 'So this is where you're hiding, Hayes! Thought you'd run away to somewhere safe, did you? I see you've decided to do some decent army work after all.' It was the CSM, hair bristling more than ever, chest heaving.

'This is nothing to do with the Army!' Edmund stood to face the sergeant-major. 'I'm just trying to make sure these poor creatures are treated like human beings.'

The CSM turned to the soldier with the Red Cross armband. 'Don't trust him. He's a conchie.'

The other man's voice stayed quiet. 'He's doing a good job, whoever he is.'

The sergeant-major glared and stamped away. Edmund bent over the next body, opened the tunic and began to read. 'Aitken O. P., 108563, New—' He heard his voice catch. 'New Zealand Division.'

He lifted his head in the streaming rain. He gazed along the line of motionless shapes ahead. Dear God, he thought. What am I going to find?

But there were only two more New Zealand names among the dead, and Edmund knew neither of them. When the last body had been recorded and covered, he and the other soldier rose stiffly to their feet. The rain was falling more steadily now. Both of them were wet through. The other man tucked the notebook into an inside pocket and nodded to Edmund. 'Thanks, chum. You're all right.'

Edmund gazed along the line of still forms. Then he moved to one of the broken bushes lining the low bank and snapped off a couple of branches. He moved along the row of dead young men, placing a sprig of green leaves on each body.

He'd just finished when the two soldiers who'd taken him from the bomb dump appeared again. 'Sergeant-Major wants you.'

The burly CSM was standing in a small side trench. On the duckboards at his feet, there sprawled a figure in uniform, with no pouches or helmet. Sodden hair was plastered to his scalp. The back of his tunic and shirt were torn to shreds, and blood oozed from cuts and scratches all over his back. He lay still, dragging in slow breaths.

'This is the conchie who wouldn't walk when we told him to,' grunted the sergeant-major. 'So we gave him a free tour of the duckboards by dragging him.'

'And you hurt him,' said Edmund. 'That was brave of you.'

At the sound of Edmund's voice, the sprawled figure moved. He levered himself over, gasping as he did so.

The CSM was shouting. The rain beat down. Edmund didn't hear one and didn't feel the other. The man on the ground stared up. His bruised face broke into a smile. 'Hello, young fellow,' Archie said.

He'd spent time in an army camp in England, too, Archie told Edmund. In the north, on a cold, empty plain. There was one part of the camp where soldiers who'd been badly wounded were sent to recover, and Archie had made friends with some of them.

182

'They'd suffered awful things,' he said. He and Edmund were seated together, both handcuffed to the wooden posts holding up the wall of a trench. The sergeant-major had ordered it. 'Leave them here so they can cry on each other's shoulders.' The soldiers had put the handcuffs on, but gently, and just a few minutes after the CSM stamped away, one of them came back with two sheets of tin. Holding these above their heads with their cuffed hands kept off the worst of the rain. It was still driving down, and the bottom of the trench was still ankle-deep mud. But Edmund felt strangely contented as he squatted there. I'm not alone any more, he told himself.

There were soldiers in the camp who had lost legs and arms from artillery fire, Archie said. Others with bullet wounds in the face. 'They look like monsters now, poor young devils.' Edmund remembered the soldier he'd seen back in England.

'It turned me more against war than ever,' Archie went on. 'Up until then, I went with the soldiers when they told me to, let them lead me around the camp to be shamed in front of the troops – just like you were, young Edmund. But after that, I decided I wasn't going to obey *any* army commands. So now they have to carry me – or drag me – everywhere.'

Archie grinned, then winced as he rubbed his neck. 'I always tell the blokes doing it that I'm sorry to cause them trouble. They usually don't mind. You get a few who are a bit rough, like today.' He held up one arm; the tunic sleeve was torn and blood-stained. 'I think my back isn't looking too good, either.'

'It's shameful!' If the CSM were there, Edmund felt he'd have hit the man. He swallowed, tried to push down his anger. If I turn violent, he told himself, I'll be no better than the war I am opposing.

Archie was speaking again. 'Well, I upset the sergeant-major. He asked me if I was the sort of traitor who wanted the Germans to win. I told him I didn't want either side to win; that it would only bring hatred from whoever lost. So he knocked me down.'

Edmund squeezed his hands into fists. He stared at the trench wall in front of him. The rain fell. The artillery crashed in the distance. Rifle and machine-gun fire was becoming more frequent again. But for the two men, it all seemed far away.

Archie sighed. 'They threw me in a cell one time. There were soldiers in there – young blokes who'd deliberately shot themselves in the hand or the foot so they wouldn't have to fight. You know what happens to them? The Army puts them on trial, and sometimes they're executed by firing squad.' He shook his head. 'I don't seem to be having such a bad time compared to them.'

184   They were both silent.

But if they were quiet, the world around them wasn't. Artillery from both sides had begun firing more frequently. The trench walls shook: water and dirt streamed down the sides to join the liquid mud in the bottom. Archie and Edmund were standing now, to keep clear of the water. At least they'd been able to slide their handcuffs up the post supporting the wall.

They ducked as a shell burst not far away, and waterlogged clods of earth flew through the air. Machine-guns snarled nearby, and rifles spat. Orders were yelled, although they couldn't make out the words. Were the Germans attacking now? If they were caught in an enemy attack, they'd be helpless. They couldn't even run.

'I helped with some dead soldiers,' Edmund said.

Archie watched him and nodded. 'Go on.'

'That's all. I helped cover them up. Made them decent. But it was army work and I did it.'

Archie smiled. 'Sounds like good human work to me. Nothing to be worried about.'

A long burst of machine-gun fire made them both jerk. More rifles were firing. More yells and a scream came to them. Edmund swallowed. 'What's happening?'

Archie sighed again. 'More bloodshed. It just goes on and on.'

185

'There are New Zealanders fighting near here,' Edmund said. 'They . . . some of them were among the dead I helped cover up.'

Archie nodded. 'It's why they brought us to this part of the line. To humiliate us in front of our own people.

And to show *them* what happens if you stand up for peace.'

Edmund hesitated. 'My brother – William – he could be here.'

Archie stared. 'I'm sorry. I'm so sorry. But it's—'

Sloshing feet approached. The soldiers who'd handcuffed them to the post, two, three hours back came around the corner of the trench. 'We're moving you blokes. No silly stuff, all right?'

'What's going on?' Edmund asked, as the handcuffs were undone, and he stood, rubbing his wrists, back and shoulders which were pulsing with pain.

The soldiers were flushed and excited. 'Our lads captured a big stretch of German trenches. Now the Huns are trying to get them back. It's pretty hot stuff up in front.'

For a second, Edmund felt almost jealous. Other men were out there, doing amazing things. William might be among them. While he—

One of the soldiers interrupted his thoughts. 'CSM wants you with him. Didn't say why.' He looked at Archie. 'You going to help us, chum? Don't want to drag you like those other blokes did.'

Archie was easing his cut, bruised shoulders under the ripped tunic and wincing as he did so. 'I'm sorry. I—'

'Just this once, Archie,' Edmund said. 'It's these fellows who have a rough time if you refuse. Wait 'til we're where that CSM is. He's the real problem.'

The older man frowned. He began to shake his head, then stopped and shrugged. 'Very well. But this doesn't mean I'm obeying any army orders.'

'Suits me, pal.' The soldier grinned. 'Don't enjoy obeying most of them myself. OK, let's go.' He raised his voice as more artillery slammed and a volley of rifle shots cracked somewhere up ahead. 'Keep your heads down. Sounds like the Huns are in a bad mood. I'll put the cuffs back on you before we get to the CSM.'

They set off along the trench, feet sucking in the porridgy, ankle-high mud. Archie didn't speak, and Edmund knew that his fellow CO was annoyed at what he'd done.

More firing and yelling burst out ahead, and he shuddered. Wouldn't this horror ever end?

My Dear Mother,

If you ever receive this letter, you will already have learned that I am dead. I know you have dreaded hearing such news ever since I enlisted, and the only regret I feel is the pain it will cause you.

I have spent the last few months with the finest group of chaps I could ever have known. We have fought for a cause we believe in and we have stood up to things until the very end. I hope that makes you feel I haven't died in vain.

I send all my fondest love to you and Jessie. I know my sister will grow into a fine and lovely woman, and she will always be there for you. Please give my best wishes to Mr Parkinson at the factory, to all our friends and neighbours, and to Violet and the others at the tennis club. I have been grateful to know you all. You may also receive a letter I left with Mr Darney before I went away, but this is the one which says what I really feel.

Mother, I want to send my love and kindest thoughts to Edmund. I have thought over and over about the choice he made. Although I still see things differently, I understand much more now about why he and others like him refuse to fight.

War is very different from what I thought.

I still feel it was right for me to enlist, but I accept and respect what my brother has done.

I've been incredibly lucky to have you for a mother. I couldn't have wished for a better life. And if this letter never needs to be sent to you, then what a lot of beautiful words I've wasted!

Your Loving Son

William

William

William had written the letter as 3 Platoon waited to march up to the trenches once more. When he'd finished, he wrote his mother's name and address on the front, and put it in the pocket of his army greatcoat that he would be leaving in the reserve lines. If the worst happened, then whoever went through his gear would know where to send it.

The five days 3 Platoon and the others spent in the rear lines were supposed to be a rest time. But they had hardly any rest.

Every night, they had to carry supplies up to the front trenches: ammunition, duckboards, food. They moved in darkness so the Germans couldn't see, but even so they weren't safe. Enemy artillery sent shells raining down. Machine-guns spat bullets suddenly, hoping to hit supply parties like theirs.

One night as they waited to move up, the enemy guns opened fire without warning. Bursts of flame shredded the darkness on the rough road they were meant to travel. Half an hour later, soldiers from 1 Platoon came struggling back, helping moaning comrades, carrying slumped bodies.

In the mornings, they worked on the roads still further back, filling the holes that long-range guns had torn in the surface, trying to heave capsized lorries and wagons back upright.

Labour battalions toiled on the road as well. Africans or Chinese from British colonies, allowed to work but not to fight. Jack Kahui shook his head. 'Do they think it's only white blokes who make proper soldiers?'

In the afternoons, they grabbed a few hours' sleep. Every evening, Mr Gowing or Sergeant Molloy inspected them, examined their weapons, made sure nobody was sick, even checked their feet to make sure the days spent up to their knees in water in the trenches hadn't caused infection. 'See,' Jack told Jerry. 'Just standing still gets you into trouble in the Army.'

On the fifth day, they didn't work in the morning. 'Holiday for you horrible little men,' Sergeant Molloy grunted. 'Get some rest.'

William, Herbert, Jerry and Jack exchanged glances. 'I know what that means,' muttered Herbert.

He was right. That night, they marched up to the front-line trenches to join the attack.

The dark came early. Clouds had begun filling the skies from mid-morning. They trudged slowly, weighed down again with belts of extra ammunition and boxes of Mills Bombs.

All around them on the narrow road columns of men and horses plodded forward. The animals' hoofs were padded, their mouths held with bridles and bits to stop them from neighing. Hundreds of troops, thousands of them, all moving towards the battlefield.

The night was quiet. A few distant guns; a couple of bursts of rifle fire far away. But mainly just the tramp of feet heading for the trenches.

William's platoon, along with 1 and 2 Platoons, left the road after two hours' marching and started across shell-torn fields. They'd gone only a hundred yards or so when the first drops of rain fell. 'Bloomin' wonderful,' muttered Jerry. 'A nice swim to the front. We'll—' He stopped as Sergeant Molloy's voice growled, 'No talking!'

But the rain eased after only a few minutes. And this time the guides were waiting and knew exactly where to go. They were led down steps like last time and through a labyrinth of trenches, all crammed with men.

William glimpsed side passages full of ammunition and Mills Bomb boxes. He stared as they edged past a stretch of duckboards where a body was being dragged along, back bumping and scraping on the rough surface. No, not a body. The man's eyes were open, and he was biting his lips against the pain. 'What's—?' William began to ask. But then they were turning down another trench, and the man was behind them.

There was coloured tape pinned along the sides of trenches: red in some places, green in others. Their guide was evidently following the green tape. They stopped after another half-hour, in a length of trench that could almost have been the one they'd spent six wretched nights in the week before. But now there were new duckboards underfoot and a fresh line of filled sandbags stacked along the parapet.

'This is it, chaps,' Mr Gowing told them. 'Sentries posted right away, please, Sergeant Molloy. Just one hour on, three hours off. Get as much rest as you can, men. I'll tell you more when I hear anything.'

William was in the second group of sentries, from midnight until one. Before and after, he couldn't sleep. He couldn't eat, either, even though he knew he needed energy for what was coming. 'No smoking,' Sergeant Molloy reminded them. 'Snipers can see a cigarette fifty yards away.'

He and Herbert leaned against the wall of the trench, with Jerry and Jack next to them. Mostly they were silent, although sometimes they talked quietly about what they'd do when the war was over. William thought about the letter tucked inside his army greatcoat. He thought of Jessie, his mother, Edmund, Violet.

Somewhere around 4 a.m., Mr Gowing came along the trench. 'We'll be attacking at 6.15 a.m. exactly,' the officer told each group of men. 'There's a mine going to be exploded under the German lines at 6 a.m. Our artillery will lay down a barrage straight after that, and we go then. Keep your heads down until you hear the whistle, then over the top and spread out, just like we've practised. Good luck, lads.'

There was silence after he passed. Then Jerry said, 'This is it. At last!' William heard the excitement in his voice. He didn't say anything. He didn't know whether his own voice would sound excited or afraid.

They were issued with extra clips of bullets and with two Mills Bombs each to carry in their belts. A dixie of hot, sweet tea arrived. Men chewed on tough army biscuits. 5.40 a.m. The sky to one side was paler at the edge. A shower of rain swept past, then stopped.

5.50 a.m. Ten minutes until the mine was supposed to explode. William imagined the British tunnellers, digging for months probably, as quietly as they could, through the earth towards the German lines, then hauling in explosives. What would it be like?

He kept swallowing. His heart thumped. He wiped sweaty palms on his trousers. 'All the best, chums,'

Herbert said quietly from beside him, as they stood by the trench wall. The four of them shook hands. Jack was murmuring to Jerry, patting him on the shoulder. These are my friends, William thought. Please let them be all right.

5.55 a.m. Everything was still. No artillery. No rifle fire. William jerked as something sailed high above. A bird. In the east, the sky had turned a dull grey.

6.00 a.m. The mine? William held his breath. Nothing. 6.01 a.m. Silence. Why wasn't— Then out in front of them, the world erupted.

A colossal roar split the air. Huge shafts of white and red fire leaped skywards. The ground under their feet lurched and bucked. In the dawn half-light, William glimpsed earth hurtling up in great fountains. Silhouetted against the flames behind, posts, concrete slabs, twisted shapes that must be men somersaulted through the air.

The noise was monstrous. He saw Jerry crouched, hands over his ears, mouth open. William realised his own hands were clamped to his head.

From behind them, every British gun seemed to open up at once. The sound blasted and bellowed. A rolling thunder of explosions rose from the ground ahead, as shells fell in a deluge on the German front lines – or what was left of them after the mine. Poor devils, William found himself thinking while the torrent of high explosive kept on. Poor devils.

Then Sergeant Molloy was shouting at him and the others. 'On your feet! Ladders ready! Wait for the whistle!'

They stumbled up, clutching their rifles, the long bayonets glinting. William bowed his head, tried to pray. A whistle shrilled. 'Over you go!' Sergeant Molloy yelled. 'Over and spread out!'

Jerry was already leaping up the ladder and over the parapet of sandbags. William followed him. Next second, he was out of the trench and advancing across No Man's Land.

Lines of barbed wire lay ahead – high coils and twists of it, nailed and looped around posts. Straight in front of him, a narrow gap had been cut. Someone's done that during the night, William realised. Figures were already rushing through, spreading out into a line on the far side. Jerry, face lit with eagerness; Jack, tense and watchful. William sprinted after them.

Behind them, whistles kept blasting. 'Spread out!' NCOs yelled. 'Five yard gap. Move forward!' Already there was a line of 3 Platoon, Herbert on William's left, Jack and Jerry further along, Mr Gowing nearby. Their officer held his pistol. The others clutched their rifles diagonally across their bodies. They began striding towards the enemy lines.

Just fifty yards in front, shells still pounded down on the enemy trenches. There can't be anyone left alive there, William thought. They're all dead.

Then a man on his right stumbled, dropped his rifle, fell face-down on the earth. And suddenly the bullets came whipping, whining and cracking as they passed, flicking up spurts of dirt in the growing dawn light. Some Germans were alive and shooting back.

A voice close by was mumbling 'All right, all right' over and over. William realised it was himself. He gripped his rifle until his knuckles turned white. Only thirty yards to the enemy front line. The line of exploding shells in front stopped, then began falling again, another fifty yards ahead. The artillery barrage was rolling forward.

A shell-hole in front of them. A glimpse of bodies sprawled in the bottom. They scrambled around it, panting under the weight of ammunition and gear. They formed their line again, hurried on. William's helmet felt heavy and clumsy. Just twenty yards to the enemy lines.

Others were all around him. Yet he felt almost alone in the shrieking waste of No Man's Land.

A whine as a bullet sped past near him. Then a grunt from his left. William turned his head sideways, and Jack was falling, the rifle slipping from his hand, blood pouring from his neck. He crumpled slowly, almost gracefully, onto the smashed earth.

'Jack!' yelled Jerry. 'Jack!' He stopped, pulled at his friend's elbow. No movement. The body lay limp.

Jerry lifted his head. His eyes were wild and staring. 'No!' he groaned. 'No!' Then he levelled his rifle, bayonet pointing straight forward, and he was running, running and screaming, straight at the enemy trenches.

The rest of 3 Platoon followed him, yelling and howling, just like they'd done at bayonet practice. William was shouting, too: 'Jerry! Jerry!'

The red-head took no notice: he raced towards the German front trench, still screaming. Next second, William saw him leap over the parapet, bayonet angled downwards, and disappear from sight.

He was there, too, just three seconds later, peering down into the trench, breath rasping, back prickling. This part of the German defences was a shambles. The rear wall had collapsed from the mine blast, and house-sized slips of earth had poured in. William shuddered as he saw an arm sticking out from under one slip, fingers curled.

Other bodies in grey uniforms lay twisted on the duckboards or sagged up against the walls. A couple of men were trying to crawl away, towards a bend in the trench, around which other figures were fleeing.

William saw it all in one glance. Then other men from his platoon were jumping down, still yelling, stumbling and rushing after the retreating Germans. They vanished around the corner. The crack of rifles and the crash of Mills Bombs split the air.

But William's eyes were on Jerry. A German soldier was crouched on the floor of the trench, arms wrapped around his head. William's friend was advancing on him, rifle raised and bayonet ready to plunge. The German saw him, gasped, tried to crawl away. He was unarmed, William saw. Jerry stepped nearer, lifted the rifle so the bayonet was directly above the man's body. The German cried out: *'Nein! Nein!'* The blade began its downwards thrust.

'No, Jerry!' William flung himself forward. Jerry hesitated, just for a second, then William's arms were around him, heaving him sideways. The two of them thudded into the wall of the trench.

Jerry twisted himself free. His eyes were slitted; his teeth bared. For a moment, William thought his friend was going to bayonet him instead. Then Jerry dropped his rifle. He hunched over and began sobbing.

For a few seconds, William crouched beside him, one arm around his chum. A yard away, the German stared at them, eyes wide and frightened. He was just a boy, William saw – no more than seventeen or eighteen. Edmund's age.

William let go of Jerry, who stayed slumped against the side of the trench, dragging in long gasps of air. As William straightened up, the young German began trying to edge away again. Once more he gasped: '*Nein!*'

'It's all right,' William said. 'I'm not going to shoot you.' The German still looked terrified. William turned his rifle so it was pointing away from the boy, and shook his head. He tried to smile.

The German's eyes were fixed on him. He let out a long, slow breath, and some of the fear went from his face. 'Stand up,' William told him and gestured with one hand.

He'd take the boy back to the New Zealand trenches, make sure he got safely sent away as a prisoner. Somewhere in Germany, there must be a mother worrying and praying just like his own. 'Stand up,' he said a second time and smiled once more.

The young soldier scrambled to his feet. His mouth trembled, but he tried to smile, too. '*Danke,*' he mumbled. 'Thank.' Uncertainly, he held his hand out to William. '*Ich*—'

A rifle shot from up the trench. The German stiffened, staggered. His mouth opened, his eyes stared at William. He made a noise in the back of his throat, then fell in a heap on the duckboards at William's feet.

Another soldier from 3 Platoon stood with a smoking rifle where the trench turned a corner. 'You all right, chum?' he called to William. 'Looked like that Hun was all set to have a go at you.'

William said nothing. While the din of artillery, rifles, and shouting, screaming men swirled all around him, he stood and gazed down at the dead young enemy. This isn't right, he thought. This isn't right.

Finally he stooped, crossed the German's hands on his chest, then turned to where Jerry still huddled against the wall of the trench. 'Come on, pal,' he said. 'We'd better get moving.'

The Germans had all retreated, those who hadn't been captured or killed. When William stared over the rear wall of the trench they'd captured, he shivered. The mine had blown a crater deep enough and wide enough to bury an entire ship. Sour-smelling smoke rose from it. The twisted metal and shattered concrete of pillboxes lay scattered around.

Prisoners were being lined up to be taken back to the New Zealand lines. They were haggard and shocked. Eyes stared from frightened faces. They and the dead young boy still lying on the trench floor didn't look anything like the savage Huns William had heard about when he enlisted.

Their own wounded were already being helped back across No Man's Land. The dead were carried by stretcher-bearers. Mr Gowing, a blood-stained bandage on one hand, paused as he came down the trench, and spoke to William, Herbert and Jerry. 'Sorry about your chum, lads. Jack Kahui was a good soldier and a fine chap.'

William and Herbert both nodded. 'Thank you, sir.' Jerry stood, staring out across the ruined land behind the German trenches, the vast mine crater, the smashed pillboxes and the barbed-wire tangles on the far side. He didn't seem to hear their platoon officer. He hadn't spoken since he'd collapsed in tears in the trench.

Sergeant Molloy was barking at them. 'Dig! Get some sandbags up on this rear wall! The Huns will want their trench back. There'll be a counter-attack any minute. Look lively!'

Men began shovelling up earth that the mine had hurled into the trench, filling a pile of empty sandbags they'd found in one corner, stacking these on top of the back wall, facing where the enemy had retreated. Others were scooping up dirt with shovels, their helmets, their hands, piling it along the parapet while others thumped it down hard. 'Leave a space for rifles!' their sergeant ordered. Twenty yards up the trench, a group of men struggled with a heavy machine-gun the enemy had left behind, heaving it up and carving a ledge out of the trench wall so that it could be turned against its previous owners.

Now that the fury of the attack was over, William felt tired to death. He wanted to flop down in the dirt at the bottom of the trench and sleep. He didn't care if the Germans came storming back at them; didn't care if he lived or died. But he made himself dig like the others. If he gave up now, it would only be harder on his pals.

Their own artillery was still firing, trying to prevent the enemy from getting organised, William supposed. Fountains of dirt lifted into the air, eighty yards or so ahead of the trench they'd captured. Black smoke drifted across the ground. It was bright daylight now, but the explosions and smoke meant he couldn't see where the Germans had retreated.

Then – 'Here they come!' someone shouted. At the same moment, William saw shapes emerge from the smoke. Men, running and stumbling towards them. Men in differently-shaped helmets from theirs, carrying rifles, tripping and falling on the churned-up ground, standing and advancing again. The enemy.

203

'Pick your man!' Sergeant Molloy was bellowing. 'Fire when ready!' From either side of William, the rear wall of the captured trench began to spit flame.

The next ten – fifteen? – minutes passed in a blur. William aimed, fired, worked his rifle bolt to eject the spent cartridge and ram in a new round, aimed and fired again. He didn't want to see if he hit anyone. In his mind, he kept seeing three faces. Jack, laughing and joking. The German boy, a second before he fell. Edmund.

The attackers had no chance. The rifles of William's platoon and the others, plus the captured machine-gun, cut them down when they were still forty yards away. They couldn't cross the great pit of the mine crater, had to skirt around it on either side. Crowded into the narrow strips of ground, they were almost impossible to miss.

William glimpsed four or five of them fall as the machine-gun sent bullets spraying across them. Somewhere along the trench, a horrified voice kept shouting: 'Go back! For God's sake, go back!'

The shooting stopped. The battlefield was silent, except for the background rumble of artillery. A few men in grey were running back to where the attack had come from, bent over to avoid the shots that didn't come. A few more dragged themselves across the ground, trying to find the shelter of the nearest shell-hole. Elsewhere the enemy dead lay sprawled, some on their sides, some on their backs as if gazing up at the sky.

William drew in a long breath. He leaned his forehead against the cold earth of the trench wall. When he turned, Jerry was staring at him, face pale and mouth trembling. 'I – I didn't think it would be like this,' the red-headed soldier mumbled.

William shook his head. 'Me, neither.'

After another few hours, fresh troops came forward to hold the trench that the New Zealanders had captured. Irish soldiers, who stared at the mine crater and shook their heads at the German dead scattered across the ground.

'God in Heaven,' one of them said, as he stood between William and Herbert, peering out over the parapet. 'You Kiwis are terrible men.' William was too weary to reply.

Rain was falling again as they trudged back over the ground they had charged across just five or six hours ago. Their heads were bent. Their boots squelched through the clinging mud as they picked their way among shell-holes and tangles of barbed wire. Stretcher-bearers were all around, kneeling to hold a water bottle to the mouth of a soldier whose leg was a wad of bandages, supporting a man in a blood-stained tunic who cried out as they lifted him, carrying away limp bodies. William wondered if Jack was still lying where he'd fallen. Beside him, Jerry and Herbert walked in silence. Once, Herbert rested a hand on Jerry's shoulder. 'All right, chum?' The younger soldier plodded on, saying nothing.

After another five minutes, they were back in the

trenches where they'd huddled before dawn, trenches now filled with other soldiers. A sour smell lingered in some places, and William felt his throat rasp. There must have been a gas attack.

They filed around corners and up steps onto an area of ground where a row of still shapes lay, each of them wrapped in an army blanket. Someone had placed a sprig of leaves on each body. William gazed at them, and felt his eyes fill.

As they reached the rough road up which they'd marched the night before, a long, sleek car drew to a halt beside them. An officer with red tabs on his collar, a stout man with a bristly grey moustache, stepped out. Sergeant Molloy and Mr Gowing instantly snapped to attention, and saluted.

'Well done, you fellows.' The officer's voice was rich and confident. 'You showed those Huns what a true Britisher can do, eh? Jolly good show!'

Jerry was just in front of William. He stiffened, and William knew that his friend was about to burst out at the newcomer. He reached forward, seized the other soldier's shoulder. 'No, Jerry,' he said. 'Don't.'

Jerry's head drooped and he trudged on again. 'Splendid effort,' the officer said once more as they passed. 'A real victory.'

A victory, thought William. A frightened boy staring and falling, a friend dead, dozens of others shot down or blown to pieces, wounded or maimed. And what had they done? Gained fifty yards of smashed earth and captured a hole in the ground. Victory wasn't what he thought it would be, either.

He trod on, rain beating on his pack and helmet, soaking and darkening the uniforms of those ahead. The artillery was firing harder again, a steady crash and boom, ahead and behind. Lines of men were coming the other way, burdened down with gear, faces tight and strained. The killing wasn't over yet.

PART 7

SECOND ATTACK

Edmund

The rain drove down as Archie and Edmund and their escort sloshed along the trench. It bounced off the helmets of troops struggling past, crashed onto the duckboards – except where those duckboards were already hidden by rising yellow water. But they couldn't hear it; it was drowned out by the thunder of artillery, the roar of explosions in front of and behind the trenches, the crack and rattle of rifles and machine-guns.

The CSM stood near a big dug-out into which stretcher-bearers were carrying silent or moaning shapes, slithering and slipping on the slushy ground. He was soaked through: beneath his helmet, the bristly hair was plastered to his forehead.

He scowled as they arrived. 'You two lend a hand with the wounded. You're not good enough to lick their boots, but I've got no real men to spare.'

Edmund ignored the insult. 'I'll do it. Not because you ordered me, but because there are people who need help.'

Archie meanwhile was shaking his head. 'I'm sorry. I won't accept any military order.'

The sergeant-major's face tightened. He took a step forward, lifted a fist. Before he even knew he'd done it, Edmund pushed between the two men, chest to chest with the CSM. 'Stop that! I said I wouldn't let you treat *me* like a dog. You're not going to treat my friend that way, either.'

The CSM glared into his face. 'I'll knock you *and* this other coward into a pulp. I'll—'

'Sarn't-major! Captain wants you, sir!' The call came from outside the dug-out. The CSM stayed glaring at Edmund for a second, shoved him backwards so the handcuffs caught at him. He lurched against Archie and they both almost fell. 'Put them to work!' the sergeant-major grunted.

To Edmund's astonishment, the escort were grinning. 'Well done, chum,' one said. 'He's a bully. Time someone stood up to him.'

Archie was annoyed. 'You didn't need to do that. I can look after myself. I told you I'm having nothing to do with army orders.'

Edmund still held the older man by the arm, where he'd grabbed him after the sergeant-major's shove. 'This isn't anything to do with the Army. This is just doing the decent thing.' How strange, his mind was telling him meanwhile. Suddenly I'm the one in charge.

211

He smiled at his friend. 'Look at you. You're worn-out. We all are. We need to help one another. Please, Archie?'

Archie said nothing. The rain thrashed and the sounds of battle beat all around. 'He's right, pal,' one of the escort said.

Archie shrugged. 'I'll do it this once. I'll do it for you.'

The handcuffs were taken off and they were left alone. Alone except for the stretcher-bearers struggling back and forth with the loads they carried into the dug-out. They huddled together against the side of the trench, out of the worst of the sweeping rain. Edmund pictured the bomb shelter and how he'd crouched there, sure he was going to die. If I ever get back home, he thought, what stories I'll be able to tell.

He realised Archie was talking, mumbling as they crouched together. 'I'm afraid, lad. I'd thought that the ones who gave in and agreed to be stretcher-bearers and medical orderlies had lost their courage, that they weren't true to our cause. Now I've found that the only way *I* can carry on is to refuse every order. But I'm still afraid.'

Edmund squeezed the older man's shoulder. 'Everyone is. The soldiers, us. Everyone has different ways of handling it. Nobody could be braver than you.'

A roaring, howling sound above made them duck and stare up. Edmund glimpsed dark shapes rushing through the sodden sky. 'Aeroplanes attacking.' Sure enough, a few seconds later, more explosions and firing came from the direction of the German trenches. Archie shook his head. 'It won't ever end.'

Another line of troops crowded past, floundering and falling in the mud, clutching rifles and bayonets, all heading towards the front line of trenches. The rain was driving down harder than ever.

A different noise came. A rumbling, clanking sound, from somewhere in the rear. 'A train?' Archie said. 'No, can't be. There's no railway lines near here. The artillery fire has smashed them.'

A voice from the dug-out hailed them. 'You two! Over here!' Archie and Edmund struggled to the entrance and groped their way down into the half-darkness. Fifteen or twenty men lay crowded together on the wet duckboards. In the dim light of two lanterns, others with Red Cross armbands were bent over them, cutting away blood-soaked clothes, tying bandages, murmuring words of comfort.

The man who'd called them looked coolly at Edmund and Archie. 'You're the COs? Well, make yourselves useful. Get some water. There are men here desperate for a drink.'

For the next hour, they toiled alongside the medical orderlies. They carried mugs of water from dixies in the corner, held them to trembling mouths. They helped lift limp bodies from stretchers as they arrived, laid them down as gently as possible. They wiped mud from faces, held smashed limbs as bandages were wrapped around them. The wounded lay white and silent, or cried out suddenly with pain. Archie murmured to them. His voice seemed to help; they grew quieter and less distressed.

Edmund, arms and back still aching each time he moved, stared into every face as it was brought in. William: was he–? He held his breath suddenly as a voice called from the dug-out entrance. 'The New Zealanders? Anyone know where the New Zealanders are?'

The man who'd told Archie and Edmund what to do replied: 'Further along the trench. They were in the first attack.'

The soldier outside moved on. 'God help them if they're in this attack, too,' the other man muttered as he bent over a stretcher. 'The Huns' artillery will know the range to a few yards.'

They'll be all right, Edmund told himself as he fetched more water. They have to be.

'Listen!' another orderly said. 'The planes have gone.'

Work paused for a moment. It was true. The gunfire continued, but the snarl of aircraft engines had stopped. Then – 'What's that?' someone else said.

The clanking, rumbling sound came again, louder

this time and getting closer. 'It's tanks!' another orderly exclaimed. 'Armoured tanks!'

Edmund and Archie gazed at each other. Tanks? What—?

Then everyone ducked at once. The thunder of artillery swelled suddenly to a deafening roar. The dug-out shook. Yellow slush from the trench splashed down the steps. Once again, whistles shrilled from all directions. Through the gunfire, shouts faintly came. Machine-guns hammered beyond the front lines.

The noise grew until it throbbed like the sound of mountains falling. The rumbling and clanking of the tanks, or whatever they were, pulsed through it all.

'There they go!' The orderly next to Edmund was shouting, but Edmund could barely hear him above the din. 'Get ready!'

Inside half an hour, the stream of wounded became a flood. Stretcher after stretcher appeared at the dug-out entrance, the bearers filthy and gasping for breath, rain pouring off them as they struggled down the steps. More figures were lifted, whimpering or crying out or silent, to lie beside the others. The dug-out was over half-full now.

Archie and Edmund brought still more water, held still more bleeding limbs. As they helped carry another agonised young man, Edmund gazed fearfully into his face and saw only another stranger. Archie suddenly said, 'You were right. This is the decent thing to do. Thank you.' Edmund squeezed his friend's shoulder again.

They all crouched as a shell landed somewhere nearby, and the ground shook once more. 'Oh, God!' a voice shouted from somewhere along the trench. 'The stretcher party!'

Edmund's stomach lurched. The CSM's mud-smeared face appeared for a moment in the dug-out entrance, glared around, mouthed something lost in another burst of gunfire and disappeared.

Edmund struggled after him, pulled himself up the steps into the trench and stared. Wounded men were everywhere, limping along supported by their friends, plodding past with bandages over faces, slumped against the walls as they dragged in breath. These were the ones who could still move, who could try to make their way to other First Aid Posts in the rear. Edmund found himself peering into their faces, too. Still no sign of the one he hoped and dreaded to see.

216

Two men came staggering towards him. Edmund's breath caught. These *were* faces he knew: from the stretcher party. 'What—' he began.

One man stared at him, shocked and shaking. Blood dripped from his left hand. 'Shell. Just in front of us. Got Henry and Ned, and the poor sod we were carrying.

They hadn't a chance.' He reeled on.

Another stretcher party appeared. Just three of them, the man at the back trying to grip both handles. Edmund recognised the thick-set figure of the CSM. He squeezed forward, rain beating on his head, and seized one side. The sergeant-major, chest heaving, glanced at him, opened his mouth, but said nothing. Inside the dug-out, they moved the wounded man onto the ground. The place was almost full. 'Come on,' the CSM grunted. He and the other two stretcher-bearers moved off again.

The dead, Edmund thought suddenly. Where are the dead? He jerked as a voice answered and realised he must have spoken aloud. 'They're out there in No Man's Land,' the orderly told him. 'They have to wait. The living first, then the dead.'

More wounded arrived. The rain poured down. The gunfire drummed on. The artillery sounds different, Edmund thought. There aren't as many guns firing.

He paused for a second, lifted his head to listen. Others were doing the same. The soldier who'd first called them into the dug-out spoke: 'The guns will be sinking into the mud. It happened before when they attacked in weather like this. Every time they fire, they drive themselves deeper in the mud. They can't shoot straight. They'll hit our own blokes if they're not careful.' The man looked around at the huddled figures, the flickering lanterns, the shadowy, exhausted orderlies. 'The attack's a shambles.'

More noise at the entrance. 'Bearers!' a voice called. 'We need more stretcher-bearers. Hurry!'

Edmund heard himself answer at the same time as someone else. 'I'll go,' they both said. It was Archie who had spoken. The two of them gaped at each other. 'You stay here,' Edmund told his friend. 'You look half-dead already. No need to finish the job.'

'No, I'll—' Archie began. Then he stopped. 'You take care, young fellow,' he said.

The other Red Cross orderlies nodded at Edmund. 'Good luck, chum.' Next minute, he was heading up the steps and into the trench.

218 Three other men waited there, two of them holding a stretcher on its side. Its canvas was filthy with mud and blotched with blood. Their sunken eyes watched Edmund as he emerged. 'Thanks, pal,' one said. 'Let's go.'

Along the trench they stumbled, squeezing against the wall as armed troops, walking wounded, other stretchers crowded by. Abandoned or smashed equipment and gasping, hurrying figures were everywhere. Above and ahead, the roar and howl of battle went on. The rain pelted down; everything was drenched and fouled with mud. Edmund remembered the man in the dug-out: 'The attack's a shambles.'

Around one corner they floundered, then another. Edmund was already struggling for breath. His arms and shoulders throbbed with pain. Then a trench wall and a ladder were in front of them. One of the other bearers turned. 'We look for the badly wounded only. If they can walk, they look after themselves. If they're dead, the poor sods stay there 'til later. Keep your head down.'

One by one, they clambered up the ladder and clawed their way over the parapet. Edmund was last, heaving the heavy stretcher up ahead of him. He hauled himself over the top, and, still on hands and knees, he stared around him.

Mud. Mud and shell-holes and smashed barbed wire and sandbags lying twisted in the filthy slush. Then his breath caught. Not sandbags – men. Some motionless, some squirming on the ground like maggots. Over to one side, black and broken stumps of trees. About fifty yards in front, a storm of erupting earth and billowing black smoke where shells were landing. Somewhere in there, men were fighting and dying.

'Come on!' They began struggling across the ruined ground. A whine, a shriek: they flung themselves face-down in the mud as a fountain of fire and dirt burst from the ground nearby.

They battled on again, slipping and falling. The din was so dreadful that Edmund thought he would be deaf forever. This was terrible. This was as bad as the Field Punishment – almost.

Two of the bearers crouched over a shape on the ground. 'Chum!' One of them pulled at the figure's arm. 'Hey, chum! Can you hear us?' No sound, no movement. The bearers looked at each other and shook their heads. They stumbled on, bent almost double. A machine-gun rattled nearby. Distant yells and shots sounded in front. The noise never stopped.

Edmund half-slithered into a shell-hole. He grabbed a log sticking out from the side and pulled himself back up. Only as he stood did he realise the log was a body. Just in front, the others had stopped by another shape on the ground, a shape so caked in mud that Edmund didn't realise at first it was a man. 'Chum!' the bearers shouted again. 'Hey, chum!'

This time, the shape stirred and made a sound. 'Take him,' one bearer said. They placed the stretcher on the mud and began lifting the soldier onto it. 'We've got you, pal,' one of them panted. 'You'll be all right.'

They didn't carry the man back to the trench.

The mud was too thick; up to their knees in places. Instead they pushed and dragged their stretcher-load across the ground like a child's sled, scooping the half-liquid slush away from the front with their hands, sliding and falling. The man lay still now, but every so often he made another noise. Edmund couldn't make out his face under the filth caking it, but he felt sure the soldier was shorter than his brother.

Another whine and shriek. Another eruption of fire, not far away. Wet dirt whipped past them, landed on the wounded man. They crawled and struggled on, pulling and shoving their burden.

Finally, the trench was just ahead. Two of them wriggled over the parapet and down the ladder. Edmund and one other bearer pushed from behind; arms reached up and seized the handles. Other troops grabbed the sides of the stretcher, and dragged it into the trench. Edmund half-climbed, half-fell over the edge and was down in the mud beside it.

Gasping and heaving, they carried the man to the dug-out. The air inside was dank and foul-smelling, smoky from the oil lamps. A medical orderly bent over the stretcher. 'Well done, you blokes,' he told the bearers. 'We can save this one.'

Edmund and the other three men stumbled out into the trench. They slumped down against the side, eyes closed, chests heaving. They hardly noticed the trampling boots of still more troops thronging towards the front line. All around, the bellow of guns went on. Will the world ever be quiet again? wondered Edmund.

One of the other bearers offered him a cigarette. Edmund shook his head, managed to mumble 'No, thanks.' The man gazed at his plain khaki uniform, no badges, no markings. 'What lot are you with, chum?'

Again, Edmund shook his head. 'I'm a conscientious objector. The Army put this uniform on me.' The soldier who'd offered him the cigarette glared. 'So why are you doing this, if you've got such high and mighty ideas about war?'

'My ideas aren't high and mighty,' Edmund told him. 'They're just mine. And I'm doing *this* to try and save lives, instead of destroying them.'

The man who'd challenged him was silent. What a time to be having a discussion like this, Edmund thought. He almost laughed, and felt a shudder run through his aching body. He was close to breaking point. He and most of the others around him. How much more of this could a human being stand?

Another five minutes and they set off again, along the trench, clawing their way up the ladder, sliding over the trench parapet into the howling waste of No Man's Land, stumbling forward as they searched for more wounded.

These men are heroes, thought Edmund, as he snatched a glance at the grunting, struggling figures beside him. I hate what they belong to, but they're heroes.

A mud-covered bundle on the ground was trying to crawl back towards the British lines, collapsing after just a yard. 'All right, pal!' one of the bearers bawled above the rolling roar of the guns. 'We've got you!'

Once more they loaded a groaning man onto their stretcher. Once more they turned and laboured in the direction of their own front line. They hurled themselves flat as yet another shell came shrieking down to land close by, then got to their feet and hauled, pushed, dragged their burden on.

The porridgy mud was so thick, it took them nearly half an hour to cover the thirty or so yards back to the parapet. Hands from below reached up again, easing the stretcher down into the trench. They tumbled after it, collapsing on the filthy ground as they tried to recover breath and strength. They blundered on to the dug-out.

But this time when they laid the soldier down, a different orderly bent over him, shook him, put his ear to his chest and listened. 'Sorry,' he said as he straightened up. 'He's gone.'

'He can't be!' protested the bearer who had challenged Edmund. 'He was moving.'

The orderly shook his head. 'He's gone. Not your fault.'

Edmund stared at the despairing faces of the other three bearers and felt his own body sag. Why were they trying to do this? What was the use of it?

Somehow they started out for a third time. They'd saved one life; perhaps they could save another. They were halfway to the ladder leading out of the trench when they had to squeeze against the wall while another stretcher party struggled past. One of the bearers was the CSM, urging the others on. The thick-set figure saw Edmund, and his mouth flopped open again in astonishment.

Something was different this time. Edmund realised it as soon as they crawled over the parapet. The noise was less. The artillery had mostly stopped. So had the rifle and machine-gun fire from up ahead. Shells still burst across No Man's Land, but the battle seemed to have worn itself out.

However, men continued to stumble or crawl across the churned-up earth and around shell-holes while the rain thrashed down on them. Voices still called out for help; sobs and moans came from all around.

They'd gone thirty yards over the ruined ground when a voice yelled 'Hey! Hey, over here!' A soldier staggered towards them, holding one arm. His tunic sleeve was torn and blood-stained. His smoke-blackened face was crowned with blood also. Or was it his hair? 'Over here!' the man kept yelling. 'Quickly!'

'You can get back by yourself, pal,' one of the bearers told him. 'Keep heading that way. They'll look after you.'

The soldier shook his head. He clutched his wounded arm harder and clenched his teeth. 'Not me – my friend. He's over here. He's hurt bad.'

They squelched after him, hauling the stretcher. Just inside the rim of a shell-hole, a mud-covered shape lay, helmet beside him, silent and unmoving. Edmund's heart went heavy. Another death.

But as they knelt beside him, the man moved. His eyes flickered, then shut again. He was so caked with mud that his face was like a black mask.

'Head wound,' said a bearer. 'Let's get him back.' As they began to lift the limp weight onto the stretcher, the soldier who'd called them tried to help. He bit back a cry as his wounded arm flopped to his side.

'Leave it,' one of the bearers told him. 'Go on – get yourself back. We'll bring him.' The soldier hesitated, touched his friend's shoulder, then set off, hunched and lurching, through the pelting rain towards the front line.

Edmund and the others struggled after him. One of them slipped in a mud patch, and the stretcher tilted wildly until they heaved it back level. Edmund was so exhausted that he wanted only to collapse on the flooded ground and lie there forever. Somehow he dragged himself on, sliding their load across the surface where they couldn't carry it, pulling himself after it.

Other wounded men reeled past. The trench edged nearer. The mud-caked, unrecognisable figure on the stretcher moved and moaned once more. Please let this one live, Edmund thought.

Into the trench they slid and dropped, fighting to keep their burden from falling. Other hands seized the stretcher and steadied it. The soldier with the wounded arm appeared, yelled something at his friend, vanished again.

They trudged and squeezed on towards the dug-out. All around them, men stood or sprawled, filthy and haggard. I'm still alive, Edmund marvelled. The man they'd brought back . . .

Inside the dug-out, Archie was helping to unbutton a blood-soaked tunic. He glanced up as they stumbled in, and stared. What do I look like? Edmund wondered, while they lowered the stretcher to the ground. There was scarcely room for another man. The lantern cast long shadows on the dirt walls. Orderlies stooped and knelt over the crammed figures, bandaging, washing, talking.

'Good pulse,' said one, as he hunched over the man they'd just brought in. 'Wash some of that mud off, will you, chum. Let's get a look at things.'

Edmund realised the orderly was speaking to him. He glanced around, saw a bucket half-full of bloody water, a rag hanging over the edge. As gently as he could, he wiped caked dirt from the man's forehead. An ugly, jagged gash ran from beside the nose, beside one eye and up into the hair.

'Looks worse than it is,' the orderly muttered. 'He'll be OK. Get some of that filth out his nose and mouth. Let him breathe properly.'

Edmund dipped the rag into the bucket again, squeezed it, washed the man's mouth and nostrils. Mud and caked blood came away. The mouth opened, croaked a half-word.

'It's all right,' Edmund told him. 'You're safe now.' He dipped, squeezed, began to wipe once more. The mud on eyelids and one cheek sluiced off, and a face was in front of him.

The sounds of battle outside stopped. The world went still, except for the hammering of his own heart. He realised the orderly was asking him something.

From across the dug-out, Archie called 'Edmund? What's wrong, friend?'

He didn't answer. He couldn't. He knelt there, unable to move or speak, staring down at the man opening his eyes beneath him.

William

William's platoon and the others had less than three hours' rest, sprawled in the shell-wrecked skeleton of a barn, a few miles back down the road. They slumped among the fallen bricks, too tired to make themselves comfortable. Some slept, but every time William closed his eyes, the faces of Jack Kahui, folding quietly to the ground, and the terrified young German, beginning to hold out his hand in the trench, were in front of him again.

Finally he sat, staring into space. The rain still drove down, dripping through the torn roof of the barn, puddling on the earth floor. The guns thundered, ahead and behind. Beside him, Jerry hunched, rocking backwards and forwards, looking at nothing.

William rested a hand on his friend's shoulder. 'Take it easy, pal. There was nothing you could do.' Jerry didn't reply. On his other side, Herbert half-lay, face drawn and filthy. 'Will's right, chum,' he said. 'We three have to look after one another now.'

The voice of Sergeant Molloy echoed through the barn. 'Attention to the officer!'

'Stay where you are, chaps.' Mr Gowing looked more exhausted than any of them. The bandage on his hand was stained with blood and dirt. 'Time to check your gear. We're moving back up to the line in half an hour. We've had orders to capture a stretch of trench just along from the one we took this morning. We need to make sure the Huns can't come at us from the side. No time to bring reserve troops up. This has to be done quickly.'

'Why?' Heads jerked as the voice came. It was Jerry, struggling to his feet, face tight. 'What's the point of it, sir? You said yourself that Jack Kahui was a good soldier and a good man. How many others have we lost? Now they want us to lose even more, just so they can have another hole in the ground!'

The red-haired soldier's voice was harsh and wild. William reached up to pull him back. He'd been thinking the same thing, but to say it out loud . . .

'Sit down, O'Brien!' Sergeant Molloy shouted. 'Sit down, or I'll put you under arrest!'

Mr Gowing lifted a hand. 'It's all right, Sergeant.' He spoke quietly, but they could hear him even above the guns. 'I know how you feel, O'Brien, but it's not our job to question orders. Things are happening all over the battlefield. We may be attacking here to help our fellows break through somewhere else. Those in command do the best they can.' He paused. 'You fought splendidly this morning, O'Brien. All of you did. I'm asking you to fight splendidly again.'

'Sir.' Jerry stared at the ground.

Sergeant Molloy lifted his voice. 'Right, check your rifles. A hundred rounds of ammunition per man. Two Mills Bombs. They're outside. Get moving, then!'

Across the muddy floor of the barn, men began to stand. William pictured the officer with the red tabs on his collar who had hailed them so cheerfully as they trudged back. Was he doing his best, too, like Mr Gowing said? How would they ever know?

Engines suddenly snarled above them as they filed out of the barn and began lining up on the road. Men ducked, began to lift rifles. Dark shapes with circles of red, white and blue on their wings swept out of the clouds, then vanished into the rain, heading for the front lines. Aeroplanes. A minute later, explosions and machine-gun fire could be heard. 'They're bombing the Hun lines!' someone called.

More noise. Different engines, clanking and growling. Around a bend in the road, a shape lumbered into view. A steel wall, higher than a wagon, thick metal treads running in a loop along its sides, machine-guns poking from slits, a bigger gun thrusting forward. Another appeared behind it, then another, rumbling through the pouring rain. Tanks. William and the others gaped as they crawled past. How can anyone stand against such monstrous things? he wondered.

Mr Gowing shouted above the noise. 'They can go straight through barbed wire, crush enemy trenches. Everything's being done to help us, chaps!'

Five . . . six . . . eight. The tanks ground on, no faster than a man marching, but growling unstoppably along the narrow road and fading into the rain ahead. From the direction of the German lines, the aeroplanes came skimming back, one of them trailing black smoke. The things I'll be able to tell Edmund if we ever meet again, William thought.

He took a deep breath, tried to grin at Jerry standing beside him. Five minutes later, heads bent as the rain drove down harder, they were sloshing back along the road, towards the front line they had left such a short time before.

They passed clips of ammunition to one another as they marched. Those who had Mills Bombs handed one to those who didn't have any. There weren't enough to go around.

'The generals are in a hurry,' said Herbert as 3 Platoon trudged through the spreading puddles. 'Hope they've had time to think this through properly.'

'I wouldn't mind waiting for a couple of years while

they do,' grunted someone from further back. Nervous laughter rippled along the ranks. William kept his head down so the rain didn't drive into his face. Will I ever be properly dry and warm again? he wondered. Just ahead of him, Jerry plodded on. He'd said nothing since his outburst to Mr Gowing. Maybe he was too tired to speak. William's eyes felt like filled sandbags. His back and shoulders ached; his soaked uniform chafed his skin.

Inside an hour, they re-entered the maze of trenches. Other troops were also trying to get forward to the front lines. Everywhere was a cram of men and gear. Stretcher-bearers struggled back with their silent or groaning loads. William didn't dare look at the faces.

Wounded men lay in every dug-out. William remembered the row of bodies with a sprig of leaves laid on each one. Whoever had done that understood that human life meant something.

'Hurry up!' Sergeant Molloy kept urging. 'Hurry up!' It's all too soon, William thought. They're rushing us into this. The artillery was building up once again. A rolling thunder of explosions filled the sky, from which rain continued to pour.

They reached a section of trench just like the morning's trench. 'Quick!' Sergeant Molloy was calling. 'Bayonets fixed! Find the nearest ladder. Hurry!' Gasping and panting, William and the others crowded along, boots sinking into the shin-deep slush of the trench floor.

One man slipped, fell face-downward, clambered to his feet trying to wipe the filth from his rifle.

Mr Gowing was shouting at them, too, staring at the watch in his hand. This is going to be a mess, William thought. We're not ready for this.

Overhead, the drum-beat of guns grew louder and louder. German artillery was firing back. As they crouched against the trench wall, they felt the ground shuddering with explosions. I hope those tanks do their job, William told himself. We'll need everything we—

Whistles shrilled. Men scrambled for the ladders, swarming up, hurling themselves over the parapet and into No Man's Land, ready to spread out and advance, just as they had that morning.

But William saw instantly that it wasn't going to be anything like the morning. The chest-high tangles of barbed wire in front were almost unbroken. Nobody had cut them, the way they had before the first attack.

They bunched there, trying to see a way through. Enemy machine-guns were already firing. William heard the *whip-whip-whip* of bullets flashing past. We're sitting ducks, he realised. They'll shoot us to bits.

Men began scrambling along to one side, slipping and falling, searching for a way through. Then Herbert yelled, 'Use me! Use me!' Still gripping his rifle, he crossed his arms over his face, floundered forward, and threw himself down across the wire. Those near him stood stock-still for a second, then they charged forward, too, clambering and trampling over the bridge formed by Herbert's body, blundering onwards.

The rain blinded them. Mud from a shell-burst showered over them. William wiped his eyes half-clear as he struggled forward. He couldn't see more than a few yards in front. The trench they were supposed to attack was invisible in the downpour, the flying wet earth, the smoke and explosions up ahead. It's hopeless, he knew. Hopeless.

Something had happened to their own artillery. The wall of fire that protected them as they advanced in the morning wasn't there this time. Far fewer shells were landing where the German trenches must be.

William wrenched his head around, trying to see Jerry. No sign. And Herbert – was he still sprawled across the barbed wire behind them? He must be cut to ribbons. Surely—

His feet skidded from under him and he fell. He hadn't seen the shell-hole. He clawed at the side as he slipped down, fingers digging into the mud. His rifle jerked from his grasp, and he grabbed it just in time, jamming his boots into the slippery slope to hold on.

He lay there, helmeted head just above ground level.

Mud and smoke and a couple of shattered trees were all he could see. And bodies. Bodies in mud-coloured khaki uniforms, lying still or crawling on hands and knees. Other men were still trying to advance, wrenching their feet out of the ooze, battling forward, falling again.

Where were the tanks? Why weren't they attacking, crushing the enemy lines? Then William heard an engine revving wildly. He stared sideways through the rain and smoke, and saw one steel shape, bogged in the mud, tracks spinning, gun pointing at the sky. A whine, the flash and crack of an explosion. He hunched down in the shell-hole. When he raised his head again, the tank lay silent and smoking. Its tracks had stopped turning.

He began dragging himself upwards, scrabbling at the slushy earth. His rifle snagged and as he glanced down to free it, he glimpsed something half-floating in the scummy water at the bottom of the shell-hole. A body.

A hand seized his arm and hauled him to his feet. Jerry, uniform sodden and torn, face filthy with mud. A little further on, he saw Mr Gowing, stooped over a fallen soldier. There was no line of attacking men, the way there'd been this morning. Just a jumble of 3 Platoon and others, fighting their way through the terrible mud, while rain and shells kept falling.

Even as William straightened up, machine-gun bullets came snapping past, a line of fountains erupting from the slush near him. A man two yards away spun sideways, fell, didn't move again. Everywhere William looked, the ground was strewn with dead and wounded.

'Come – on!' Jerry was bawling in his ear, but William could barely hear him above the roar of artillery and the crack of rifles. He stumbled forward again. His boots were balls of mud; wrenching one from the swamp of No Man's Land seemed to take all his strength.

Somehow he kept moving. That morning he'd felt weirdly alone on the battlefield. Now, there seemed to be dying or panting men all around him. And everywhere the noise of the guns, like great monsters bellowing.

They hauled themselves around another shell-hole, coughing as smoke blew past. A body lay in the bottom of this one, too. No, a figure desperately trying to climb up the sides. Then an explosion, a fury of flying earth that sent them staggering sideways, and when William peered down again, the shell-hole had half-collapsed, burying whoever was in it under masses of mud.

He heard a different sort of cry. A soldier had turned, was trying to run back to the trenches they'd started from. William glimpsed a terrified white face, eyes wild and bulging. The man had broken under the horror of it all. Next minute, Sergeant Molloy had the soldier, yelling into his face, wrenching him around towards the German line, somewhere ahead in the smoke.

For a second, William seemed to see and hear

everything at once. The wasteland of rain and mud, blackened tree-stumps, shell-holes, wrecked machines and wrecked men. The screams of voices and falling shells. The foul smoke and deafening explosions. This isn't heroism, he knew. This isn't war. This is Hell.

Still no sign of Herbert. The enemy line seemed to be about thirty yards in front. Would they ever make it? Rifle and machine-gun fire grew louder with every step as they battled forward. A burst of bullets split the air to one side, and William hunched over, head sunk into his shoulders.

He straightened up again, and his back went cold. Jerry was hit. His friend lurched sideways, hand clamped to his right arm. Blood was already pouring out, soaking the sleeve of his tunic. His rifle dropped. He stood swaying, staring at William. His lips moved, but no sound came.

238 William threw himself through the slush to Jerry's side. With strength he never knew he had, he seized the torn tunic sleeve and ripped it apart. Blood streamed from a deep gash in Jerry's upper arm. A glint of white bone showed.

Amazingly, the First Aid lessons of months ago in their New Zealand training camp were instantly in his mind. From his own tunic pocket, he snatched the tightly wadded field dressing, shoved it hard into the armpit on Jerry's wounded side. 'Keep your arm – down against you!' he told the dazed soldier. 'It'll help – stop the bleeding.' He grabbed Jerry's field dressing, too, tore it open and wound the bandage as hard as he could around his friend's arm. Straight away the bandage was blotched with red, but the flow of blood seemed to be less.

'I'll find help. You sit here!' He pushed the red-head down onto the ground.

'Be – careful!' grunted Jerry through clenched teeth.

William straightened up again and stared around. In the space of just a few minutes, the attack seemed to have stopped. On all sides, men were moving back, turning to fire behind them as they stumbled along, helping others, slipping and falling in the mud. William saw Mr Gowing, one arm raised and signalling, revolver gripped in his fist.

He saw stretcher-bearers, too. Four of them, three with Red Cross armbands, labouring through the mud twenty yards away, heaving their heavy stretcher. 'Hey!' He began to yell as loudly as he could over the storm of the guns. 'Hey! Over here!'

They hadn't heard him. William struggled towards them, gasping and shouting. 'Hey! Over—'

An ear-splitting shriek rose suddenly behind him.

As he started to throw himself down, a white flash erupted on his left. A wall of heat slammed at him. A bellowing roar dinned in his ears. At the same moment, someone smashed him across the head with a steel bar. He felt the blow on his helmet, heard it ring like a gong with the impact. His head swelled with heat and noise. Hot rain gushed over one eye.

He reeled sideways, trying to understand. Somehow an enemy soldier had crept up and attacked him. But how – he tottered in a circle, trying to see and protect himself, peering from one eye. There was nobody near.

Jerry, he told himself. I have to get help for Jerry. 'Hey!' he shouted again. It wasn't a shout; it was a croak. His legs wouldn't hold him up. His head seemed to be filling with darkness. From somewhere far away, he watched himself crumple down into the mud.

Thunder was rumbling above him, William realised. And rain was falling on him. He must have been caught in a sudden shower while he was walking to work. No. No, he was on the battlefield. He was lying down, for some reason. He had to get up. Jerry . . . that's right, he had to get help for Jerry.

But his legs wouldn't work when he told them to, and his head kept throbbing. His helmet – what had happened to his helmet? I have to get a stretcher party for Jerry, he remembered now. He tried to call out, but his mouth wouldn't work, either.

Strange things were happening to the daylight. It kept going dark, growing bright again, then fading once more. He felt so tired. He could easily go to sleep right there on the soaked ground. No, he told himself, I mustn't do that. There's something I have to do first. Jerry . . .

Faces drifted in front of him. His mother and Jessie. Edmund: he had to talk to Edmund, too. Violet from the tennis club. He'd made his mind up – when he got back home, he'd ask Violet if . . .

His head felt hot still, in spite of the rain. Hot and different, somehow. He tried to open his eyes, and see where the stretcher parties were. His eyes *were* open, but he couldn't see anything. Was he—?

He *could* see something – just. Men, hurrying, staggering back towards the trench they'd started from. There was Mr Gowing, helping one along. Should he salute? he wondered. No, I'll look silly, lying on the ground and saluting.

Nobody seemed to notice him. It didn't matter, William decided. I'll just lie here and go to sleep. Or die. Dying didn't seem to matter, either. The light grew bright, then started to darken once again. Everything was fading, further and further away. I'm cold, he realised:

cold and soaked through. I really should go inside and change my wet clothes. What will Ma say if she sees me all filthy like this? She'll really give me a telling-off.

'William! Will!' That was his name. He must be in school. No, he was in the training camp, and somebody was ordering him to get up. He tried to say 'Yes, sir', but his mouth was half-full of mud.

'Will!' He knew that voice. He tried to speak again, managed a croak. Next second, Jerry was there, staring into his face, eyes wild and frightened. Jerry looked different, too. There was a blood-stained bandage on his arm. William remembered that bandage. Hadn't he . . .

'Are you all right? Will?' Again he made a croaking sound, tried to nod his head. But his head felt twice its normal size. And it hurt. It really hurt. Why hadn't he noticed that? Hammers pounded inside it.

Jerry's face vanished, and another one was there. A man he'd never seen before. 'Head wound,' he heard the man saying. No, it's Jerry's *arm* that's wounded, he wanted to tell them.

'Can't see how bad,' the man was telling others. 'All that mud. Let's get him moving.' Then hands and arms were all around him, lifting him, lowering him onto something. A stretcher. This is wrong, he wanted to tell them. The stretcher is for Jerry. I'm – but noises and sights and the world were going dark and distant, like they had before.

Gaspings and gruntings were what he heard next. He was rocking, lurching from side to side. A boat? No, he remembered – the stretcher. Men were carrying him. His head still hurt. Hurt badly, but it didn't matter. I've seen war, he thought. I know war's a mess. That's what matters.

Words were being spoken. William couldn't hear them properly. Couldn't hear the guns properly either, but he knew they weren't firing so much. Everyone must be going home. Won't that be wonderful?

He could see from one eye. The other felt glued shut. Rain was still falling on him, but it was good and cool. The sky looked dark and low and sodden. He could make out the stretcher-bearers' arms, as they clutched and staggered along. Khaki tunics, one with no badges on. Helmets and bare, wet heads.

He rose up, so suddenly that he almost cried out. Then he was dropping down, down, and more hands and arms were all around him. He glimpsed clay walls on either side, men pushing past. Some glanced at him; most just plodded along. He was in the trench.

Jerry's face thrust at him. His friend was all right, even though William hadn't helped him. Good.

'Herbert—' William tried to understand what Jerry

was saying. 'Herbert . . . safe.' That's good, too, he decided. He felt himself being carried again. More exhausted faces passed by. Their attack must have failed. Somehow he knew that. It was another thing that didn't matter.

Once more, the world faded to blackness. When things came back, it was still dark, except for a dull glow near him. An oil lamp. He was in a shelter or a deep trench of some sort. Another strange face was looking into his. It turned away and said something to another figure nearby.

Then cool water was on his head. A cloth was wiping him, gently, carefully. William kept his eyes closed. The mud was slipping away. His skin felt clean and good. He wanted to thank whoever it was. He opened his mouth to speak, but his lips were still caked with dirt, and could only mumble.

'. . . all right,' a voice said, as the cloth wiped wonderfully again. '. . . safe now.' William felt the world stop. He knew that voice, too. He listened, but it didn't say any more. Nobody was speaking or stirring. Everything had gone still.

He forced his eyes open and gazed up. Then he knew that even though he felt awake, he must be dreaming, or even dead. Because the shocked, disbelieving face of his brother Edmund was there. Edmund, a wet cloth clutched in one hand, staring down at him.

William and **Edmund**

Four hours later, the two of them were on their way to a rear First Aid Post, where William would be treated and then sent to hospital. A line of stretchers threaded slowly along the trenches, carrying blood-stained figures. William lay on his back, head covered with bandages, gazing at the sky. Edmund held one of the stretcher handles. Whenever they stopped, he stared down at his elder brother. Sometimes he rested a hand on William's shoulder, as though to make sure he was really there.

The soldier who'd guided them to William on the battlefield had appeared again just before they left the dug-out, one arm in a sling. 'Sergeant Molloy says you have to get well fast,' he gabbled to the wounded figure. 'He says they need someone to look after me!' He took William's hand in his unhurt one, then turned to Edmund. 'And *you* look after *him,* chum.'

Edmund smiled. 'I will. After all, he's my brother.'

The red-haired soldier's eyes looked as if they were going to pop out of his head. 'Brother? What – How – Who – Why?'

William managed a half-grin. 'I'll tell you later, Jerry. Come and visit me, pal. I'll try to find you some pretty nurses.'

In the moments after their gaze met in the dark, echoing dug-out, both William and Edmund seemed unable to move. For long seconds, they stared at each other. Then they were both exclaiming at once. 'William! You're alive!' 'Edmund! Is it you?' Their hands met, clasped, held. Words poured from them, without their knowing what they said.

Archie came stooping over to see what was happening. 'This – it's William,' Edmund managed to say. 'My brother. It's him! My brother!'

Edmund's friend stared. Then a smile spread across his face, and he shook his head. 'Dear God. Who would believe it?' He reached down and took William's other hand carefully in his. 'You should be proud of this young man.'

William spoke, weak but clear. 'I am. I'm very proud.' Edmund began to smile, felt something on his face, and realised he was weeping.

They told each other a little of what had happened to them. Not very much: Edmund kept being called away to help as more stretchers came in, with more silent or groaning figures. The second time he came back to where William lay, his elder brother was asleep. Edmund knelt and gazed at the filthy, blood-smeared face for a few seconds. He touched William's cheek and heard himself give a long, slow sigh.

Outside, the noise of fighting had almost stopped.

246

A few guns fired far off, paused, fired again. For the moment, the battle seemed to be over. Another figure appeared in the dug-out entrance. A young officer with a bandaged hand. 'I'm looking for William Hayes.'

Edmund stared. It was Archie who replied. 'Here. A nasty gash in the head, but he's going to be all right.'

'I'm glad to hear that.' The officer squeezed his way to where William lay. Edmund made his way over, also. William blinked up. 'Hello, sir.'

'Hello, Hayes. Very pleased to hear you'll be OK. The other chaps want to send you their best.'

'Thank you, Mr Gowing.' William lifted a shaky hand in Edmund's direction. 'Sir, this is my – my brother. Edmund.'

Mr Gowing's mouth dropped open. 'Your brother? Heavens above!' He looked at Edmund, then at William again. 'Yes, I can see he is.' The officer shook Edmund's hand and spoke the same words that Archie had spoken. 'You should be proud of this young man.'

Edmund smiled. 'As someone else said, just a little while ago – I am. I'm very proud.'

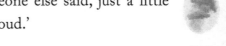

After another hour, the line of stretchers had reached the rear trenches. Already, the war seemed a little further away. Edmund had no idea whether there had been a victory or a defeat. He couldn't care. His brother was safe. Just now, nothing else mattered.

They struggled up a flight of muddy steps. The rain had gone. Somewhere birds sang. Ahead on the rough road, a line of ambulances waited, red crosses painted on their sides.

Edmund felt a hand touch his wrist. He glanced down at William. 'Did you bring my helmet?' his older brother asked. Edmund laughed and shook his head. William smiled, too. 'You always forget things.'

But I won't forget this day, Edmund knew. Not ever. He and the other bearers placed William's stretcher down carefully on the ground, while they waited for the ambulances to begin loading. Edmund sat by his brother. His whole body ached; for the first time in hours, he realised how exhausted he was.

'I'll write to Ma,' he told William. 'She'll be so relieved. Jessie, too.'

'Thanks,' William murmured. He paused. 'And could you tell Vi—'

He fell silent. After a second, Edmund glanced at him. He stared. It was hard to tell under the dried mud and blood that still covered most of his face, but he felt sure his brother was blushing.

He gazed around, at the mud, the shattered trees, the torn ground of war. He drew in a deep breath. Everything was going to be all right.

Dearest Ma,

This is not a letter from one of your sons. This is a letter from BOTH of your sons! Yes, William and I are together. Together in the same place, and together because we are friends again.

We met in the most wonderful way. I have been in the front lines of the battlefield, but I am unhurt and well. I have survived where so many brave men have died.

I was helping as a stretcher-bearer, carrying wounded troops to the First Aid Station. It was a place I hope I never see again, but I will tell you all I can about it when we meet. Or William will tell you first, which is more likely.

Anyway, one of the soldiers we were carrying was so ugly that I had to look hard at him to believe he was real. And who could be more ugly than my dear elder brother, William?

Yes, Ma, he has been wounded, but he will be all right. And he is coming home. The doctors say he mustn't fight again, and he will sail back to New Zealand as soon as he is well enough. Isn't that the very best of news?

A piece of exploding shell must have hit his helmet. I always knew my big brother had a thick head, but I never knew it was that thick! He has a deep gash along one side of his face. It will leave a handsome scar that all the girls will fuss over. Ma, the doctor says that his left eye has been damaged and may not recover all its sight. But he is alive. Alive and young and strong, and he will make his way back to health.

He sends all his love to you and Jessie. He asks you to tell Mr Parkinson that he's looking forward to getting his old job back. (Please give *my* best wishes to Mr Yee when you see him, and say I hope to be back in his garden sometime, also.) Oh, and William wants to send his best wishes to some girl called Violet. Isn't that interesting?

I'm sitting by his bed, in a hospital in France, well away from the battlefield. He needs to rest a lot while he gets better. He still finds it hard to hold a pen and write. Anyway, I was always better at spelling than him.

Dear Ma, you will see William before you see me. I don't know what my future holds, as long as this terrible war continues. But men have spoken up for me – including some men whom I thought hated me – and I may be sent to work in a hospital for badly wounded soldiers. The officer of William's platoon, a fine young man called Mr Gowing, is a doctor, and he is going to see what he can do.

There are many good people in the Army – I've learned that. I respect them, just as I respect and still believe my friend Archie. I hope the war ends soon, for the sake of all young men everywhere. (Do you remember saying that, Ma?) All young men, and all their friends, sweethearts and mothers.

Ma, I have talked so much with William (when he isn't sleeping – and snoring sometimes, but don't tell him I said that). He's told me about the places he's been, the battle he fought in, the friends he's made.

I've met some of those friends, when they come to visit. A young soldier called Jerry, very proud of the stripe on his tunic that shows he's been wounded. An older man called Herbert, who knows my friend Archie! They both belonged to the same church back in New Zealand and they were overjoyed to see each other again.

I have seen terrible things, dear Ma. I won't try to hide that. I have seen the evil that people can do – and the good that they can do.

William and I will never agree on some things. He still believes it is right to fight for your country. I cannot accept that. But he says also that he has come to believe that war should only be a last resort; a country should fight only after it has tried everything else.

Who would ever have thought that this would happen to us, dear Ma? That two brothers should believe in such different things, go such different ways, yet end up together in the same faraway place. Life is very strange.

Life is very precious, too. William and I agree that whatever happens to us for the rest of our lives, we will do our very best in the world. We will try to help others, to be true to our friends and generous to our enemies, to leave things a little better than we found them.

Big words from your small son, dear Ma. William is still asleep. When he wakes, I'll see if he wants to write a sentence – yes, even though his spelling is so bad. This chair beside his bed is so comfortable that I may sleep for a while, too. May all yours and dear Jessie's days and nights be happy and restful, 'til the four of us are together once again.

Your TWO loving sons

Edmund and William

For more great books for young adults

go to

www.aurorametro.com